maka shan

VOLUME ONE

MAKA SHAN SAGA

maka shan

VOLUME ONE

MAKA SHAN SAGA

written by
Anatarra Whitewing

afterword by
Dr. Angela Browne-Miller

Metaterra® Publications

metaterra®
publications

publisher's note

*Dedicated to those
who are on the journey
and to those who are
already there.*

Everyone.

table of contents

prologue:
resurfacing into the now

Who I am is the whisper thin fabric of wizened spirits, the fragmentation of fragile cycles in time, the waning Mother Earth's last wish, maybe. You may imagine me. You may find me real. You may be me....

Despite my (and our) intellectual resistance to this information, it appears that an ancient race of medicine women is resurfacing through time into the now. These people, or beings, are reuniting in this time for a simple reason: they are coming together to help the human species on Earth reassume its true power. And to turn time. You see, there is still time to rewrite the future of this kingdom, to save life on the Earth, to ward off the great great Great War. This is a collective consciousness type of event. We are all in this together.

I learned all this early on. This was a hefty dictum for me to absorb as a young adult, however, over the years, I have grown into it as if it were the most natural of all things, a process of personal development those who are living their callings know. Living one's calling is a large project, but it's the only game in town. What else are we doing here? Why else live? Each of us proceeds through our own levels of initiation as we unfold our own particular destinies. Those of us who are inclined to watch for signs of this magnificent procession will indeed find them. Those of us who are not watching will nevertheless pass through these levels. Listen for your calling. This is what your life is about.

I have learned that it is wise to honor the precious although often-testing initiatory steps of life. This recognition and honoring of our deeper experience is how we reveal to ourselves the invisible yet powerful thread of meaning knitting our daily experiences into coherent journeys. This is the way we quicken our souls, and establish the enduring substrate of the self. This is how we fortify that essential seed of consciousness which we can, if alert, take with us when we depart the particular lifetimes we are now living. This is how we remember who we are and why we are here.

You too are here now, at this time in the life of this Earth and her people. Think about why.

I offer the following piece of personal history in honor of your journey as well as mine as we all negotiate our great collective yet also essentially solitary pilgrimages down the great river Styx -- a river who wears many faces, and flows through many mythologies, in many forms, under various names.

Sit very still and truth rushes in. ... Open the portal and you are there ... Drink of the waters of the Goddess Styx and feel the rushing water upon which you travel....

For like rushing water nothing moves.

Maa-Kah-hoh Tehrr-ha, vozhlahz wo, mee skhan-hey-yah.

Maka, Maka, Maka Shan.

Sayeth my name
if thou wouldst
travel upon me.

Egyptian
Book of the Dead

part one:

vicious initiation

1.
sudden wind

Sometimes it is like just yesterday.

I thought it was a sudden wind, slipping in through an open window.

Instead, it was the cool rush of angel wings.

It was late 1970 and I was eighteen. Just an hour earlier, I'd been raped, or had endured something along the lines of a somewhat ritual rape, on the other side of that big door. Now I was crouching on the floor of this dilapidated Victorian house in a town in northern California. It would be several decades, and a long complex modern day career and life, before I would come to terms with the meaning and teaching of the events I describe herein. I would eventually discover many others who were also coming to terms with such events in their own lives.

Just before it all had happened, there I'd been, in my long braids, tattered shirt and faded jeans, an awkward, lanky, and naïve teenage girl, in way over my head, and seriously blind about my immediate situation. Someone down in the stairwell had been playing a protest song on a poorly tuned guitar, wailing softly against the Viet

17

Nam War. I had covered my ears, trying to think. I had been shivering, almost frozen with confusion, with no idea what to do next.

I told myself that all I had wanted by coming there was to find my boyfriend – who was Native American. He had said that, as I was Native American too, or at least part so, Tsalagee, I should be proud of this. I should not hide it the way my parents had wanted me to. One's blood should not be a family secret. He too was a young idealist, like me, in search of utopia. We wanted our lives to mean something. We wanted to help make a difference, and save the planet. And we wanted to know if we were really living in what people were calling "end times."

He had said he'd be here at this house to meet me. But he hadn't come. He hadn't been here. And I had. And then all this unraveling of all I knew and believed had happened ….

****

There were no lights on. A few candles were burning, flickering over a dreary river of clothes, army surplus sacks, dirty backpacks, moldy sleeping bags, tattered blankets, and ragged people in various stages of sleep or stupor. Then something happened in the midst of all this inaction. An unusually skinny young black girl, about fourteen, emerged from behind the big door that led into the leader's bedroom.

She walked slowly with her eyes glued to the floor. Her blouse was hanging open, revealing barely-formed breasts. She was holding up her unzipped blue jeans with one hand and trying to close her shirt with the other. Silent tears stained the side of her thin face. No one but me seemed to notice – or dared to look maybe.

I bit my lower lip as I watched the girl move directly toward me. Stumbling several times, she seemed to take forever to cross the room, as if she were walking through a thick invisible mud. Questions started chasing through my mind. I wondered if there was still time to try and get out of the building. But they had taken all my things. And could I really leave without getting stopped by the men who seemed to be guarding the doors? And should I go out into this strange neighborhood in the dark of the night? Was I more in danger out there or in here?

I took a deep breath, as silently as possible. Maybe no one would notice me. I wished hard to become invisible. Marijuana smoke wafted its way lazily, a river of illicit nectar, across the room. I tried not to feel stoned, but my head was murky. A few liquor bottles leaned against a nearby pillow. They were open, lacing the smoky air with the odor of stale alcohol.

The skinny girl from behind the big door finally reached me. She sat down facing me. For a brief moment, I was relieved. Finally some contact with another young person. I touched her knee – she cringed – and suddenly I felt horrible. My intuition started seeing bits of what was coming. My insides starting caving, collapsing to a distant center. My soul began shutting itself into a tiny box for safekeeping.

The girl started to whisper to me, slowly and in a monotone, studying each word as if she had to force herself to talk: "He told me ta' … get ya' … he wants yooo … now …." Her voice trailed off and her gaze faded to a mindless stare into space.

"What for?" I whispered, trying to sound irritated to hide my fear.

She wasn't looking at me, but she did respond. "Yoooo know …" she murmured and then she mumbled something else unintelligible.

I couldn't understand her. Maybe if she talked a bit louder. I tapped her arm and pleaded in a whisper, "What did you say? I can't hear you."

She hunched over, holding her knees tight to her chest, becoming a hopeless fetus. She turned her dead gaze toward me. "… wants yooo ta' do it."

"What if I don't want to?"

She shrugged. "Yooo just haf' ta'."

"Who says?" I demanded, my whisper cracking around the edges.

"They … don't let ya' ever leave … if ya' don't."

I didn't like what I was hearing: they don't let you ever leave if you don't? "Oh yeah? They can't make *me,*" I tried to boast.

She came alive just a bit. "Oh, yeah … they can."

No more was said. I was mad. I wanted to be mad at her but I couldn't. I wanted to help her but I couldn't. The girl unfolded, got up, seemed to sleepwalk to a pile of old blankets, and then just wilted down into them. She crumpled up like a dead bug. It was as if she had faded to nothing.

I looked around for some sign of my things. I would definitely go out into the night. The dark out there couldn't be more threatening than this, could it? I shifted position, scanning the place and poising myself to bolt. I was about to spring up and dash out silently.

But then the big door opened.

2.
big door

I can still see that door swinging open.

The few people who were awake turned their heads ever so slightly to see Fire Star, the great Chief of this newly formed clan, the Fire Star Tribe, come out. The candlelight forced his shadow to reveal itself – for a moment he and that warrior shadow were one. Then the body of the man stepped forward, unfolding his flesh out of his shadow and into the dark jungle of sleepers.

He walked toward me: barefoot, silent, and with an eerie motionlessness, as if he was stalking me. He slowly moved right up in front of me and squatted there. He waited. I studied him warily. An unusual strain of confusion came over me. He did not feel to me like he looked. I tried to reconcile this mismatch, but couldn't. These days, I know what I am reading when I get this feeling. Back then, I just felt like a confused and cornered animal.

Here, in the flesh, right before me, was the hero I had admired from afar, the radical leader I had heard so much about. My hero, Chief Fire Star, was stepping boldly into the glittery and explosive dawning of what was proclaimed by that era's hippy mainstream to be the New Age, the dawning of the Age of Aquarius. But, instead, Fire Star was declaring this the dawning of his people's return to power and the Earth's return to the hands of the true people. He said that the indigenous peoples of the world were the true keepers of the planet, and the true keepers of the true wisdom about the planet, so these people should be the gatekeepers to both the planet and its wisdom. He also called the North American indigenous people the "Red Men." He said these people should be the arbiters of power on this planet as it was they who were the chosen ones, and as it was they who had been first delivered here from the stars. Fire Star had announced that now was the time for the essential return of the great red wisdom, the red power. And, I had been very drawn to his view. I was, after all, part indigenous too, in fact even part Native American. (*Of course, it would be years later that I would wonder what peoples here on this planet were not indigenous to this Earth, but that is another story for a later volume in this series.*)

I had never known anyone like him. I could feel how very special he was. This visionary man had proclaimed himself a revolutionary tribal leader – the teacher and protector of ancient Native American survival knowledge. People said he was a special medicine man, that he could do magical things, talk to dead ancestors, read nature's signs for coming Earth changes and even apocalypses. And he sure looked like he knew some important secrets. And he sure looked like a hero, although he was older than I had expected. But this made him look wise. I didn't find him at all handsome, but he had a magnetic way about him. He was a sacred animal and he was a wizard. I could tell. He looked to me like a shaman.

I studied him as he stared at me. I had no idea that other medicine men would come to question his practices – but far too late to stop him from taking me as his own. He wore a spotted feather in his long dark hair. He had a beaded leather bag with something in it hanging around his neck. He wore a huge silver bracelet with a huge turquoise stone in it and a silver ring bearing a claw shape imprint. But what he was wearing was unimportant. He was larger than life. I wanted so very much, so desperately, to be impressed the way I had expected to be.

And I was impressed by his message. But now, feeling my spirit under siege, I wasn't able to feel so good about finally meeting him. He seemed to carry a massive cloud of fractured energy around his physical body, as if he were swimming in some kind of dark liquid full of soft but shattered glass. I didn't feel good near this energy. I didn't like it – not at all. I was confused. How could I feel this way about this great man?

"Come in now," he ordered smoothly and softly, taking my hand. I didn't like his touch. I gazed numbly at the man's thick hand on mine. And then I shivered. For just a moment, I thought I saw a bear's paw there. I was startled. Was his shape shifting or something? I blinked and the paw became a hand again.

He stood up and pulled me with him. Now it was I who looked at the floor as I trudged behind him, still feeling his firm grip on my hand.

He took me through that door and closed it. As I crossed that painful threshold, time stopped for just a second. A faint vision of some kind of event – or rite of passage – whispered itself in my mind. I remember a question asking itself of my unaware teenage mind: what am I seeing? Have I been through this before? Of course not, I told myself sternly. But I didn't have time to think about it. Survival mode was setting in. Pay attention. Watch out, I told myself sternly. I had to stay alert, alive.

Crossing through that threshold was indeed a big deal. Not that there was anything special behind the door. The place was, if anything, disgusting. I reeled at the clashing smells of strong marijuana, heavy incense, and rancid sweat. There were burning candles in rows along the walls. He had a mattress on the floor in the middle of the room. It was like a bed throne, I said to myself as I gulped.

He spoke to me in a quiet but commanding tone. "Come smoke some good medicine with me now."

He sat down and crossed his legs on the bed. Avoiding the bed, I sat obediently on the floor, facing him, also crossing my legs. I looked up at him. He reached out, attempting to hand me marijuana rolled in a special paper held by a silver clip. There were feathers and beads hanging from the clip.

"Soaked in our medicine tea, our peyote tea, special for you."

"No thanks," I said, wanting to try and stay clear, so I could think about what was happening. I definitely didn't want to do anything on this bed throne with this chief man, no matter how important to the future of the Earth his message was.

He lit the joint. He took a puff. Then he put it to my lips. "Have some now." There was an imperative in his voice.

I looked at his face, trying to think. I took a very small puff, holding the smoke in my mouth and then exhaling before it reached my lungs. Our eyes locked. I held his gaze with a numb sort of defiance. I felt a little dizzy, but I didn't look away. I summoned every bit of testy adolescent rebelliousness I could find within me.

Fire Star noted my defiant response to his gaze. "You're different, a different kind. How did you find us? What do you want here with our sacred teachings and people, with the Fire Star Tribe? … Are you the one we've been expecting?"

For a moment, I thought maybe I could get through to this man. Maybe my explanation would help. So I gave him all of it in what felt like one breath: "My boyfriend, Mark, had the address. We both thought you were doing the right thing, that you stood for something good … back to the land, against materialism, stopping all the exploitation of the planet and of the native people, teaching people survival skills, and uh, ummm, trying to save the planet from destruction and all. And Mark is half Native American – he's from Alaska. Before he left, he asked me to meet him up here and said your people would find him for me. I want to find Mark."

Chief Fire Star shook his head no. "He is not here. He is up on the tribal land."

"Well, then," I said, trying to sound as if I'd just had a great idea, "Tell me how to get to him. I'll go there."

He frowned. "That is a privilege you earn from the elders."

"How?"

"The land is sacred. You serve to enter. You serve us."

"I won't do just anything."

He chuckled like an old man and touched my hand. "Service is not just anything, young woman. It is respect. Respect for the land and the Native American people that white man has ravaged."

"I have that respect, but I didn't ravage the Native American people. You are older than I am. I wasn't born when it all happened. I shouldn't pay for it. I didn't do it."

"We all pay for the work of our ancestors. They make the world that we come to be born in."

"And then we remake it," I said, trying to reason with him in my youthful, stubborn manner.

"Our ancestors live on. They speak to us. They speak through us. They live in us. I can answer your ancestors through you." He looked around the room as if my ancestors were there.

I looked up at him seated on that bed throne. "I don't think you have that right."

"You are child of white man. A daughter. You have the privileges your ancestors stole from my people. You live on the land your ancestors raped. They brought pollution, destruction and disaster to Earth – and you are responsible."

Me? I was confused. Not me. "I want to leave now," I said – but I only glanced toward the door. Again those questions: Could I get out? Would anyone stop me? Would something worse happen if I tried to leave?

Fire Star took another puff of his pot, narrowed his eyes as if to peer into my mind, and then exhaled a gigantic peyote pot cloud around me. "Lilith, is that your name?" he asked me. "People tell me that's your ugly name."

My pulse rate shot up. "I have a lot of names," I said as nonchalantly as I could.

"Lilith, what does this stand for?" he persisted. "What kind of woman is a Lilith?" He sounded very disdained.

I shrugged. I could see he hated my name. I hoped he wouldn't hold it against me because I hated this name too. I shuddered inside.

"Answer me," he ordered. "Who does this Lilith think she is?"

"Myths or religions or something say this name is from the story of the Garden of Eden, among other things."

"What does this story say about Lilith?"

I shrugged again.

"Tell me. I know you know."

I could see I would have to answer this. "In the garden of Eden story, they say Lilith left Adam after she refused to become subservient to him. So she would not return to the Garden of Eden, she wouldn't go back to him. Other stories say she was kicked out of the garden of Eden for not becoming subservient. Adam got another wife after that, the next one was Eve of the Adam and Eve story...."

29

"Hmmm," Fire Star growled, eyeing me angrily. "Judeo-Christian bullshit."

"But really it is all just stuff to me, I'm not into all that Lilith stuff," I told him.

He narrowed his eyes and shook his wide head. "None of this is part of our story. This Lilith is not one of ours. She is no goddess of ours."

"Well, she's not one of mine either." I hoped all this would get me off the hot seat. "I just ended up with this name Lilith by chance."

"Nothing is by chance," he said severely. "You are responsible for this name."

At that moment, I wondered more than ever why my parents would have saddled me with the name of the woman who I had been told was supposedly the Biblical or at least Kaballic Adam's first wife, the woman who wanted equal access to sacred power and knowledge and was therefore cast from the Kingdom of Eden. My mother had explained this to me long ago. "I cannot help what I am named."

"We will fix this. We will change your name for you. As you come to us for big lessons, you should be called the right way. ... You will be called who you are to be." He reached out to me.

"No." I jerked away from him.

He gave me a look of severe disapproval, and exhaled another smoky cloud.

A wave of something invisible hit my mind hard. The room spun for a moment. I stopped the spinning by shaking my head. Did he just now hit my mind? No, I told myself, I am simply feeling the dizzying effects of the pot. But I knew I was wrong about this. He had some kind of mental power.

"Remember who you are – wherever you find yourself," I told myself silently, using words my mother had once said to me. But I was beginning to doubt my ability to stand up to Fire Star. My attention was being distracted – the lights and shadows in the room were dancing. Was that sensation coming from the peyote he'd said the joint had been soaked in? I had heard about peyote. It would make me see lights around the edges of things, lights I had heard were called auras. I could certainly see that darkly jagged cloud around this man more clearly now.

I was lost in my thoughts. He touched my wrist to get my attention. At first I ignored him and went on thinking about the peyote. It wouldn't be very strong taken as a tea or on a tea-soaked marijuana joint. Or would it?

He pressed his fingers into my wrist and pulled me toward him. I resisted. I told myself to hang on, stay alert, don't get sleepy or space out. Not now. Maybe you can get away still. I felt hope trickle through me. But, now, as he pushed the peyote pot joint into my mouth, I felt my thoughts slow to the speed of cement.

"Hmmmmm." He narrowed his eyes as he studied my face and then my body and then my face again. I felt like an animal being inspected at a stock yard sale. "Who are you – a beautiful young white goddess?" A mix of reverence and disgust filled his voice.

A what? What was he getting at? Why this attitude toward me? And why did he assume I was all white, whatever all white was, when I was not?

His expression showed that he felt somehow angry about this goddess thing. He seemed suspicious of me. I reacted quite defensively. "No, I'm not a goddess, I'm just an idealistic kid from suburbia who believes in you," I answered, surprised to find myself trying to hide some deeper identity I hardly knew I had. Questions stumbled through me. What was this strange and sudden instinct I felt to hide? Who was I that I would suddenly have this need to keep him from seeing me?

He looked at me sternly. "I am not here to hurt you. You should be grateful. This is a ceremony, a sacred ceremony, a passage. If you were the one in power, you would take the same."

"Same as what?" I asked although I already knew that he meant take me. My body. What he did with the skinny girl. "No, I would *not* take from other people without their permission."

"But you have for so long."

"What do you mean?"

"America is red man's land, not white man's land."

Who said I was white, I wondered but did not ask. I mean what is white, and what is part white, for that matter, I asked myself. "I already said that I didn't take America away from you. Why should I pay? I'm eighteen, not hundreds of years old."

"Why are you here?"

"I said, to see my boyfriend who, according to you, is out in the mountains in one of your communes."

"He has gone to the land, our land. Fire Star Tribe land. He is one of us, our color. He belongs there. This is his birthright. You are not of red breed. You must pay for that passage."

But I am red breed too, I said to myself. I decided not to present this right then, because it shouldn't matter. "My boyfriend loves me. He's waiting for me. He wouldn't want you to hurt me."

"I will not hurt you. This is how we come together. This is how you join our nation. You do not carry our blood. You are not one of our Tribe. You cannot be us – until I fill you with my seed."

I reeled inside, feeling disgusted and fearful but trying to remain expressionless. "And that fourteen year old girl, too? She's not white, she's black. Does she have to pay for passage, too?"

He didn't like my attitude. He frowned at me. "You ask strong questions, and wrong questions." He narrowed his eyes until they were almost all the way closed and then looked at me from between his eyelids. He studied me for several long minutes. "Hmmm," he said, "I see that someday you will be a very strong white medicine woman, a white bird, a healer, a leader into sacred realms. You will step into our sacred territory as if you belong here, but do you belong? … Hmmm … But it is true you will have a chance to get permission. Maybe, if you follow our rules, we will let you learn the real medicine from us … the real thing and not those games and lies your people play with. … We know the good medicine. Good medicine you can teach. Good medicine you can use to survive ... and to really make a difference and really heal the Earth."

I listened carefully because part of me knew part of what he was saying was very right. But what was this thing about my not having a right to be in sacred territory?

He looked me deep in the eyes with a long, penetrating glare. It was a cloaked but nevertheless violent look. I could see there was blood in his eyes – and I could feel waves of racial prejudice hitting me. I was confused. I had come to the Tribe because I felt like part of it. I felt I carried the blood. I thought I was in sympathy with the Tribe's position. I agreed that native peoples had been robbed of their rights, didn't I? I had been robbed too. So had my family.

I reeled as another but heavier wave hit my psyche. A river of red blood rushed through me from another time into that present moment. It carried images of massacred women and children, and murdered warriors. They were native people. Whites had killed them, and the carnage, abandoned by the white killers, was being pillaged by huge bears. I could clearly feel the bears chewing on the flesh, as if it were my flesh. The bears were red with the blood of the dead, becoming the spirits of the dead as they consumed them.

A deep, cellular-level, profoundly genetic, and very emotional confusion rattled through me. I was one of the massacred dead. And, at the same time, I was not. Core level conflict raced through me. For a moment I felt deeply, grievingly, apologetic. I winced with guilt, with shame – and in that very second I saw Fire Star's eyes widen and his body poise to lurch forward. He was the hunter and I was the prey. He was the captor and I was the prisoner.

No! Something deep within me cried out – I am not compensation for all those crimes! This is ridiculous! I was seething with adolescent defiance. I would not sacrifice myself for these dead of long ago! I myself was one of them! As I felt this teenage resistance to the pull of Fire Star's energy, something far more mature – eons old it seemed – welled up within me. From out of nowhere, I was filled with some sort of ancient power – it rushed into my young body and naive heart with such force that I gasped loudly. *(It would be many years before I would begin to understand this power sweeping into women in our times.)*

Fire Star's head jerked a fraction of an inch to the side with surprise. I saw that he knew what was happening within me. And he seemed to want to hide what he was knowing. He knew he was being answered with power – untrained power, adolescent power, but power to be reckoned with. There was more going on here than he'd expected. I was not like the other young runaway girls who had come through here and been in his bed at his command. Maybe he could hold me captive for now, do what he wanted with me for now – but not forever. He might take me down, but I would rise again. And again and again....

I felt the tension increase. He had recognized my power far more than I had. He had seen my future and found that I would be a formidable tribal elder – I stood for something he did not like – I had come to do something he did not want to have happen. He saw I had come to take the torch, to **challenge him for control of the clan**. Although I didn't get all this at the time, Fire Star felt threatened by my return from somewhere. I didn't understand why, but I definitely could feel him declare war on this future me, on some kind of resurfacing ancient me that I didn't yet know I had, on some kind of highly unusual purpose for my existence that I had not yet discovered. *(And Fire Star and I were merely one pair of people living out this symbolic struggle, as I would know much later in my life.)*

I stiffened inside. What was this conflict about? Flickering hints of who Fire Star and I really were darted through my psyche. I felt my posture, my face – even my shape it seemed – shift back and forth between that of a scared eighteen-year-old girl and that of a powerful ancient priestess. I was confused to the core by my state of mind, but I hid this weakness and narrowed my eyes.

It was at that moment of fragile impasse between us that Fire Star reached and lifted his rifle from the crumpled blankets. A gun? A gun! I had not seen the weapon in the dim light until right then. I felt my teeth clamp tight – but I continued to try to breathe calmly and carefully, staring at his eyes, not at his gun. I definitely did not want to show fear.

He actually raised the weapon and aimed it at me. "This is my weapon. I traded a woman for it," he said, and looked me in the eye by gazing right through the sites of the gun.

I blinked once and continued to gaze back at him. He wouldn't really shoot me, I tried hard to convince myself. This is 1970, my mind rattled. People don't just shoot women for no reason. And people certainly don't trade women for guns anymore. Would he shoot me? Would he shoot me? God, he could actually shoot me. He's high on pot and peyote.

Don't get scared now, I ordered myself with a silent but loud inner voice that I had never before heard myself use. It didn't even sound like my voice. But I had no time to ponder this. I felt a sharp quiver of fear race throughout my body. I worked hard to ignore it. I told myself that I had to detach from fear, from any emotion I might have in this situation, in order to survive. I had to be alert, and nothing but alert.

"This is my weapon," he warned again. "It is loaded."

He continued to stare into my eyes – to pour his will right into me through my eyes. Then he made a move, and carefully placed the rifle next to his leg on the bed. I relaxed just a bit. I thought he had changed his mind. We were frozen there a moment, as if someone had hit the pause button on a movie. I was about to breathe a sigh of relief when he commanded, "Come here, on this bed." He motioned me to his other side, where there was no gun.

I had to be alert and not emotional. Yet, the problem with my effort to detach from my fear and feelings was that I was also distancing my focus from the whole experience. My alertness was sinking into a stupor. I did not want to be forced to be a zombie like that poor skinny little girl had been. I noticed my vision blurring. I was having a hard time knowing what to do. I couldn't hear myself think.

But I knew one thing. The "come here" command I had just received from this man was an assault upon my dignity. He didn't think I was listening so he said it again. "Come here, on this bed. Now. I will not use the gun if you will do what I say. And you will like having me take you with my manhood more than with my gun. Woman, let me have you and you live, if not, then you die."

That cloud of energy that surrounded him expanded unexpectedly and engulfed me. And my mind, now unable to even think about any safe way to resist, shifted into a seemingly irreversible numb automatic. I felt no emotion – I stood up and obeyed his order.

As I sat next to him, I felt my gag reflex activating – a deep mechanical repulsion. I tried hard not to vomit, held my lips tightly shut – but I did vomit. It wasn't much because my stomach was empty, and I held it behind my sealed lips. It tasted terrible on my tongue. I felt the powerful impulse to spit it out at him, but I numbly, and wisely given he had a loaded gun, chose to swallow the foul stuff instead.

"Undress now," he commanded.

Frozen with indecision, I continued to resist him: I just sat still and looked down at the floor by my feet. I made no motion. He waited a few moments, then slowly reached over and, grabbing the material, pulled off my top. He pushed me, his hands on my shoulders, and I fell back onto the mattress. He unzipped my jeans, and roughly yanked them off. I was frozen. I could not make myself move. Then he removed my underwear.

With fear but also with a strong naive surge of indignation, I leveled my eyes at him, now trying to send him arrows of force – energy to force him away. I summoned all my youthful power into my eyes and voice. "You have no right to do this to me," I told him tensely, hoping against hope that the force of my gaze would back him off.

He leveled his eyes right back at me and stared at me so hard that, for a moment, I thought I would be consumed – flattened to nothing, ripped to shreds, and eaten – by his hungry energy. My heart cringed. Barely veiled, in the wilderness of the soul behind his salivating eyes, was a wild bear or something, ready to consume me.

I felt more naked than I had ever felt in my life. Undressed to the bone, unshielded, unprotected. I swallowed. I wished to God right then that someone would come in and make him stop. Then I was thinking in desperation: was the gun really loaded? Would he really shoot if I said no? Yes.

Just keep looking him in the eye, I told myself. But then, I suddenly got the feeling that it was he who was telling me to keep looking him in the eye – so I tried to break eye contact. But this seemed impossible. He had locked my gaze with some kind of invisible hook. I felt trapped.

He was touching me with his paw-like hands as if inspecting a lesser animal he was about to slaughter or to rip to shreds and eat. "You have good breasts. Nice breasts, juicy meat," he said. His rough leathery palm covered one of my breasts. "Mmmm," he moaned, "a good and white belly." He touched my stomach with his other hand

and mumbled something unintelligible. It felt as if he'd created some kind of piercing circuit running through my body by placing his two hands on key spots, one over my heart and one over my abdomen. A stream of something foreign raced through me, energy pulsing from one of his hands to the other and back. This stream seemed to be filled with microscopic razor blades that were making tiny slices in my insides.

My emotions were boiling by then, but I told myself to try and be totally devoid of feelings. I kept telling myself that I had to stay alert, to keep my head clear to see a way out. Was that gun really loaded? Could I grab it and aim it at him? Jumbled thoughts tumbled through my mind. What was I supposed to do now? Did anyone know where I was? Where was my flute? Did Mark know about this? Did I tell any one I was coming here? Was this really a sacred ceremony, and was I wrong to withhold my spirit from participation? Confusion raced through my fear. Was I the one who was wrong here?

Yes, a voice from somewhere in my head said.

No, I told myself, this is not my voice.

Yes, that other voice said.

No, I heard again, loudly. My inner voice was now filled with that ancient priestess energy, stunning me with resolution: I am the right voice: I am me, I am not wrong. What is happening is not right.

"This is very wrong," I blurted out angrily at Fire Star. "I can't believe that you of all people would be like this. You were my hero only a few hours ago."

I'm not sure that I would advise a young woman about to be raped in such a situation to express such defiance. Once I spoke this way, he became more physically aggressive with me. He shook me by the shoulders as if trying to get through to me. "Yes, I have a right, woman. Your white grandfathers raped our women and killed our men."

He was wrong, he had to be wrong. I glowered at him, trying to pose a threat of some sort.

He grabbed his gun and set it on the floor pointing toward me. Then he became very still and severe. He grabbed me harder. "I have a right."

I reached to pull his hands off of me. "Those weren't my grandfathers! My ancestors didn't rape or kill anyone!" I managed to sit up.

Now his anger amplified. Now he shook me -- so hard that it seemed the insides of my head came loose. I went limp and he threw me back down. I saw that he looked like a bloodthirsty animal. I froze. As he stood up, I made a weak effort to get off the bed but he pushed me back. He leaned over and looked down at me, ready to pounce. I froze again. Then he took his pants down but not off. I glared at his erect penis.

He narrowed his eyes and said something – some sort of chant I think – in some language I did not know, looking around as if someone else was in the room who could hear him. Then he tilted his head and listened to something, as if he was hearing an answer. He grunted and nodded a yes. Then he looked back at me, and spoke sternly to me in English.

"This will be good for you. If you look, you can see the spirits gathered here. When someday, years from now, you become a great wing, a medicine woman, you will remember this initiation ... you will remember this meeting with the spirits."

It was like an invisible crowd had gathered. I was paralyzed with fear. And I was humiliated.

He came over and down on top of me with his heavy weight. Then he penetrated me. I wanted to scream but couldn't make any sound. He started moving slowly and chanting while he did. I tried to push him off. He grabbed my arms, got quiet and moved at a rapid pace. At first it hurt me, what he was doing – then I felt no sensation. I went out of myself or something.

Without stopping, he lifted his head and looked me in the eye again. I tried to shut my eyes but there was a hook in his gaze. "Move. Move with me," he demanded in a deep voice.

I did not move.

"Move, I said," he muttered tensely with some kind of new degree of threat in his voice. On automatic, I moved in time to his thrusting.

As he began to move more feverishly, I came back into myself and realized that the pain was intense. Now I tried hard to push him off, struggling fiercely. Now his hands moved to my neck to control me. I struggled harder to get out from under him. In response, his thumbs pressed into the front of my neck, shutting my windpipe as he banged his penis into me repeatedly. I stopped struggling, but he didn't release my throat. Instead he pressed his thumbs in harder. I couldn't breathe at all. I struggled for air. He pressed still harder into my neck. I tried to gasp several times and then stopped trying.

Time seemed to suspend itself. I had no energy to panic. I had begun to taste the soft cement of death in my mouth. I thought I would die. I think I did die. At least for a while. I flew away like an angel in a hurry, my beating wings the wind sign of a great white bird ....

3.
agony to rapture

I know I left my body.

I entered a strange blankness, an empty space and hollow time. I felt as if I was waking up from anesthesia – but waking into nothingness. Questions of death flitted through my consciousness like secrets telling themselves. I don't know how long it was before I eventually looked down at myself and saw myself under him. I was not moving. Then it hit me: Dead? Was I dead? I was dead! My silent voice sounded loud in my disembodied ears. There was some kind of echo out there, an echo of my voice. Dead? Yes, dead, I seemed to decide, surprised to feel a wave of relief.

What happened in the next few moments probably happened very quickly as time is measured here on Earth. But what happened stretched itself out and filled itself up with a vast amount of timeless experience. This experience saved my life. It has never left me.

I looked down and saw myself frozen with humiliation and death. Yet, I did not feel any humiliation from up there. I remembered that I had vomited just a while before. But now I was not down there, in my flesh, to do so. I was somewhere else. Somewhere else? Yes.

There is a somewhere else! I was in another world, a world very close in to the day world, but distinctly different from it. This discovery was absolutely exalting. I was in a place full of chalky light, inhabited by glowing, living presences made of a fine dust that was composed of light-giving particles.

These living presences had faint yet very detailed faces. They had old faces, ancient, feminine, and compassionate. Why do they seem to love me? I asked myself. Why do they feel like family? Are these the ancestors? Whose ancestors? But then I said to myself, wait, why don't they do something to help me down there? Whose side are they on?

Now some other element arrived on the scene, and I felt I was somehow being pulled upon. This other element was tugging on me as if to pull me away from these presences. I became aware of a conflict between them. What? A conflict regarding *me*?

This sort of experience was a lot to deal with, especially for a recently disembodied spirit with little training or memory of training in this area. I felt lost and directionless. I wanted to panic but I couldn't figure out how to experience panic without a physical body to breathe fast, raise its pulse, and perspire more. So I just floated there, in a sort of inter-dimensional suspension shock, in the vacuum of my ignorance.

I found myself trying to think back on what had just happened – and discovered that thinking itself was, at first, weird to try to do without a body. I found myself flipping frantically through the recent chain of events. I'd been in mortal physical danger, being raped and strangled. And then, in the next moment, I was out of my body suddenly safe from the danger that had grabbed me down there in my body. And then – just as I felt the relief of death, I was, in the next moment, very unsafe out here in this unknown realm.

Confusion overwhelmed me. Imagine coming into a state of pure rapture – profound exaltation, seeing the most beautiful light possible, discovering angelic presences awaiting you, feeling the awesome ecstasy of spirit that comes with such an ascension, and then finding some kind of unexplainable turmoil out there in what a moment before looked to you something like heaven.

Somehow, I quelled my disembodied panic and pulled my energy to a new inner center I had just then discovered. Now I understood the basic problem very quickly. Some of these beings – they looked like warriors of some sort – wanted me to stay dead, not to go back to Earth and do what I had gone to Earth to do. They were attempting to catch me and imprison me – they seemed to want to kill me. "But I am already dead," I heard myself think-saying as I darted away from their spears of hot energy. I thought I heard a reply pound into my center: "Not dead enough. You must be stopped in all dimensions."

Just then, the others of those beings out there, the ones that first had greeted me, came back in. They were a very tall cluster of Seven very old, magnificently luminous, very kind intelligences. They came around me. Again, they appeared to be feminine entities – royal energies – priestesses. They embraced me. Ahhh! My center felt secure with them. I felt myself being filled with a deliciously radiant sensation which it seemed I had been longing for, for years of Earth time. Divine bliss. Divine.

But momentarily I realized, without direct words being spoken, that these luminous presences wanted something from me: they wanted me to return to that claustrophobic and painful life down there, so I could complete my life's work. This was preposterous. They wanted me to go back down there and reenter the girl's body that was being raped and strangled. Overwhelming! Cruel! I thought. What could be so important? I was eighteen – what was this gargantuan project they were handing me, I wondered.

And then there it was, in hyper-clarity – the *Work*. A hand reached out from the clustered bodies of the Seven ancient presences and handed me the Work in the form of a glowing package of intricately woven light, a downloading of highly condensed teachings, messages and plans. I recognized the package right away. I had seen it before, somewhere … sometime. I felt myself expand. The heart of my center opened, and I reached out to accept the bundle. I wasn't precisely sure what this meant, not consciously, but I agreed.

They say not to look down when you climb something too high for you. I looked down and saw a teenage girl being raped and strangled. And then I remembered I was dead. I was stunned. This can't be happening because I am dead. "Yes," I heard, "it can."

And then my spirit was spun rapidly until balancing like a gyroscope. And in the fleeting passing of this motionless spinning of this eternal yet brief balancing, the trade was made clear. They would save my life that day. They, the ancient women made of light, would make every effort to protect me from the ongoing assault of those who would try to stop the Work. And I would go back and live down there to do what I had to do in the time that was now coming. I would do the Work. There would be obstacles, there would be hurdles, there would be those who would try hard to stop me. But I would weather these tests and continue to do the Work.

I headed back, what seemed like "down," to that body which it seemed I had been out of for an eternity. And then quite suddenly, quite miserably, I was back in my flesh. I definitely felt myself re-enter physicality – I crashed back into my body.

I felt instantaneously both claustrophobic and in mortal pain. It seemed forever before Fire Star stopped banging deep into me. Then he came, blasting me with razor sharp shards of his hot fractured energy – and it was done. I felt I would surely suffocate as he lay on top of me, almost snoring, for a few endless minutes.

He finally rolled off. My body was burning and hurting and wet with his perspiration and semen. I hurt horribly around the edges, but I felt entirely numb inside – dead.

He was saying something. "You will stay in here tonight. Sleep in my bed. You are mine, the chosen one. No one else will have you. You will be stopped and shot if you try to leave."

I stared at him, my unblinking eyes those of a corpse.

He covered the space between my legs with a firm hand and said something I did not understand, something in a language I did not know. Then he placed his other hand on my abdomen and seemed to pray. I couldn't understand his words. I hated his touching me that way. My core hated it. I felt like property – his. Could worse than this happen to me? But there was no escape – I was entirely wasted. There was nothing in my body that could stand me up and move me out. Now it was this very bed of my humiliation that offered me my only comfort. Maybe I could sleep now. Deal with what next tomorrow. I looked at him without expression.

He looked back at me, unaware that I could see that the lie of his supposedly spiritual purpose was revealing itself, leaking from around the edges of his old face so haggard with dishonesty. I had returned to this life with a new kind of vision. I could see more. *(It would be years later before I would see the whole picture, and realize we were both players in a far larger process. True forgiveness would be hard to come by, but I would find it.)*

He went on talking as if he were a sage. "You have much to learn, much to understand about power ... you are safer not to try to match power. And not to tangle with the Fire Star ... the Fire Star power. Your role is woman. This is different from mine. Woman receives power, takes it in, nourishes it, holds it but does not put it out except when called upon, in service, in childbirth, and in death. You did not learn your right place from your white mother. We should bring her here, too."

I came to life a bit, feeling a dull numb rage. In my mind I said, "Do not even touch my mother with your thoughts or I will make you pay." However, the only words I could manage to whisper defiantly were, "You can't. My mother is dead."

"Mmmmm. Already an ancestor. How long?"

"Six months ago." I showed no emotion.

"And so you inherit the line … yes, you will be a woman to be reckoned with someday. But for now, woman, I have you. I will have what my power brings me. You will stay here. You are mine, you sweet young goddess. Mine."

He stood, pulled up his pants, rubbed his penis, and then closed his pants. He picked up all my clothes and his rifle and then walked out the door with them.

The big door closed.

4.

momma

It was over.

I pulled my knees to my chest as I lay devastated, naked to the core, a hopeless fetus on a stinking bed. A stream of questions staggered through me: Did I get a disease? What was that heat in my belly? Did I get pregnant? Was that the spark of new life that was ticking within me? When would he be coming back? Would this happen to me again? Could I get out before that?

I felt my drugged mind slowly falling asleep despite my efforts to stay alert. Misery began to creep into my heart like a filthy muddy flood. I pulled a dirty blanket over me. I tried to cry. I was desperate. I wanted my dead mother back so much. But I couldn't cry. I made a silent scream into the air, "Momma!" several times, demanding that time and space yield her unto me.

Eventually, I began to dream. At least it seemed I was dreaming, but I felt awake. Some time passed before I could focus on what I was seeing.

When I finally was able to focus, the seeming reality, even tangibility, touchability, of what I was seeing was startling. I saw a very old, very regal woman. She was wearing a long, tattered but intricately beaded and feathered robe, and a large hood or shawl-like piece that hung in such a way that it concealed most of her weathered face.

She came to me with a small glass box. She was right next to the bed. She looked to be some sort of very special, very wise, very ancient priestess. It occurred to me that she was one of the Seven spirits who had embraced me when I was being strangled, but I lost this thought in the face of the sharp crystalline intensity of this present vision.

She began to speak to me – speak may be the word – if this is what describes the experience of having her words filter like a beautiful healing syrup into my mind. "I am Sveeka."

Sveeka? I had never heard such a name, yet Sveeka sounded so familiar to me.

"I have traveled far … what is inside is for you," this mysterious old woman whispered melodiously.

She opened the box and took out its contents, holding it on the tip of one of her extremely long extremely old fingers: one very large drop of glistening, absolutely luminous, water, very very clear, very very pure. A water crystal.

"In this is the knowledge, the power, the Light of Truth. You have died for this before. You will again."

What? Why did this make sense to me?

"The time is coming for the Great Return. Prepare. You will continue the sacred lineage of the Seven Sisters in the ancient star way of the *Wazine Maka Shan.*"

"*Wazine Maka Shan,*" I whispered in awe. "*Maka Shan....*"

"Do not be fooled about the importance of your mission. Let no lies consume you. Lies are famine. Truth is feast. Pass this drop of Truth on many times. It will always return to you. It has always been with you. Be its Keeper. Protect this Light."

The woman leaned toward me, her finger holding the drop closer to my heart. I reached out to accept the drop, and felt a gentle current – more like a stream of light -- race through me the moment my skin touched the surface – the skin – of the water.

Immediately the drop crystallized to a soft but intricate snowflake. I put this crystal on my tongue and swallowed it for safekeeping. As I did, it gently burned a cool hole right on through into my soul. The crystalline snowflake seemed to go to my heart where it began glowing inside me like a star. Then it moved to my forehead, where it stayed.

The old woman nodded her head in approval and said, "Watch for me. I will come again when time opens. And often before that." She began to dissolve into thin air. A wind from nowhere seemed to rise and spiral up around her. The hood flapped away from her face for just a moment.

I was stunned. What? What! Is this high priestess my *mother*?

MaaaaMaaaa! Don't leave me again! My heart cried out silently – it drained itself into the room around me – it wailed mutely for my dead mother. I needed her so much. I tried to make sound, to cry out her name, but I could make no sound. I tried to reach for her, but I could make no move.

And then she faded away to a chalky wind.

I toppled. I fell a long distance, as if I'd fallen into a deep hole. But I was still on that bed in that room behind that big door. I fell and fell, deeper and deeper, finally falling into a deep, soothing, trance-like sleep. I could have been in that trance forever. I don't know. Maybe I still am. Whatever folds and wrinkles time made there in that room took me on a journey through many years ... into the past ... into the future ... and many places ... around the Earth ... into the stars. And home, home, home.

There, lying in that room in that trance-like sleep, I saw pieces of the life that lay before me. But back then, it seemed to be a dream. It has taken me years to see in that dream a mandate and a directive, a vision and a premonition of the lifetime I was about to embark upon. The catapult had been sprung and my trajectory ordained.

part two:

wisdom the hard way

5.
journey to the realm

Time suspended itself a while.

Hours later, or was it days later, in my sleep, I heard the door open and close. Someone came and sat on the bed. Somewhere inside me I felt fear, but I was too worn out to feel very much. I moved a couple of my fingers a little bit – they brushed up against each other. Somewhat surprised I was able to feel my skin, I opened my eyes, too groggy to be anything but vaguely apprehensive.

The candles were out. It was dark in the room. The window was covered with blankets. I couldn't tell if it was day or night. There was a burning between my legs that just wouldn't quit.

The person spoke. It was a man's voice. "Mark has told me of you. I've just come in from the land. I am Gun."

I eyed him warily. He was strikingly clean cut. He was younger than and dressed differently from Fire Star, but appeared to be Native American. Did he know I was naked under the blanket, I wondered nervously. Would he expect me to do it too?

"No reason to be afraid," he said as if he'd read my mind, "I am not going to do anything to you. I will take you to Mark. But we must go now. Fire Star is out for a while and I don't want to argue with him tonight. Come."

I tried to speak. At first my voice wouldn't come out. I cleared my throat and tried again. "He took my clothes," I said numbly. I wondered dully, what did this man expect me to do? Stand up naked?

"Let's go find them." He stood up. He was beautiful, tall, lean, dark-eyed, dark-haired, and very dark-skinned. He wore clean, relatively new blue jeans and a blue denim cowboy shirt. No jewelry.

At a loss or maybe just too confused for alternatives, I wrapped myself in the tattered blanket, stood up, and followed him out the door.

Everyone was asleep now. Was it the same night? I saw my clothes in a heap on the floor. I found myself thinking that my clothes looked pitiful and filthy. Then I realized that what I was really thinking was that I was pitiful and filthy. At least you're alive, I told myself, although I sort of doubted this, as I felt so dead. I picked up the clothes, looked at Gun, and tilted my head toward the bathroom door where I intended to change.

"Do you have any other things here?" Gun whispered.

"Yes, but they took them. I have a green back pack with a mandolin and a wooden flute tied to the outside."

"I'll find your things. You go dress."

A few minutes later I was dressed and walking out of the bathroom, trying not to step on any of the sleeping bodies. Or were they all dead, I wondered. The crumpled skinny girl was nowhere in sight. I found Gun by the stairs. He had my pack. "Let's go," he said. "Now."

I followed him out the door, down the steps into the drizzly night, and into a rusty blue truck. There was a bottle of apple juice on the seat. "Drink that," Gun directed. "You must be dehydrated."

He tried to start the truck three times before it gave in and revved up. He had been thinking about something. "We got the other three teenage girls out already. They're all under eighteen. Fourteen, fifteen and sixteen. Every one else around there is over twenty-one, except people's babies." He paused waiting for me to say something.

I said nothing so he went on. "We don't all agree on how to build the new Tribe. Fire Star is only one of the chiefs. He thinks it is his show, but it is not. And he thinks the sign of the Fire Star is his but it is not. This is a Pan-Tribe, a coming together of all tribes. The Fire Star is bigger than he is." Gun looked at me, a disheveled girl in long braids. He asked me, "How old are you anyway?"

"Eighteen."

"Were you one of the ones that asked for it?" he wanted to know. When he glanced over and saw that I looked confused, he restated his question. "Did you want to go to bed with him?"

Who could possibly want to bed that man – that Fire Star – I wondered as I felt shame and embarrassment rush through me. "No way, but it seemed like I had to. I mean, he had a loaded gun. A rifle."

I heard Gun grind his teeth, and I saw him grimace with great anger. He seemed to growl a moment. Then he cleared his throat.

"That is not the right way. But many of the men in this new Tribe feel that white women are theirs, a trade. They say they are carrying the old way of the old Fire Star – but the truth is, they have brought a new rage, sick with revenge, to what was once the sacred Fire Star. It is a crazy rage – dangerous for all of us."

"It's stupid," I heard myself saying. "It was so long ago that all that happened … white men taking this country from Native Americans."

"Only on some calendars. Your people and mine have different time lines. We walk in different worlds, even though it appears we stand in the same place."

"Oh," was all I had to say as I struggled internally over my racial confusion. Was I white? Red? Dead? I wasn't sure.

Gun went on, "Your people do not see our time … they do not live in natural cycles … that is why your world is coming to an end."

I said nothing to this and stared out the window. I was already dead, I told myself. So what does the world coming to an end matter to me?

While he drove, I fell asleep and slept most of the way. Hours later, as he turned the truck off the paved road and onto a rugged dirt track into the mountains, Gun saw that I was awake. He nodded at me. The sun came up. We drove in silence for quite a while and then slowed and pulled into a nondescript clearing in a scraggly wooded area.

I had never seen woods look so shabby. It wasn't just the devastation that bothered me, it was the sloppiness of the devastation.

Trees were half cut, branches were ripped off trunks, hatchet marks were made everywhere for no apparent reason, and there was old and new garbage all over the ground. So this was "THE LAND," one of the sacred areas Fire Star had named as a safe place to weather the coming Earth changes. This was one of the places where people who wanted to survive were going to build a utopian back-to-the-land community, one designed to survive the coming geologic, ecologic, economic, and political upheavals.

Gun stopped the truck. "Here we are," he murmured. "The land," he said with a hint of sarcasm. He glanced at me. Then he got out of the truck, where he was greeted by five very somber men– burly men who appeared out of nowhere. They were carrying rifles.

I climbed out of the truck. I felt my feet sting as they touched the ground. A sharp burn raced up my spine. What was this bizarre electric current coming out of the Earth here? I realized with the jolt that I was indeed in Fire Star territory, but not just any territory. I had finally set foot on the "safe land" I had been seeking, the survivor territory that I'd had to pay such a price to enter – the sacred grounds I had been forced to spread my legs and trade my flesh for.

I felt no joy at my arrival. I felt like a piece of refuse, my raped body screaming with its own disgust. I told myself the price of admission to this supposedly sacred land had been too high. And now, each of these armed men was looking me up and down – intercoursing me with his mind. And I was hit with that same feeling – of being a hunk of flesh, a prisoner slave, or an animal for sale at a market – that feeling I had had when facing the scrutiny of Fire Star. Once again, I was a thing, a body, less than a person. It didn't matter what my heritage really was, I was only white, and worse, white female, in their eyes. They were hungry, hungry for something. I could feel them consuming me. I struggled not to reveal that I could feel them doing this and that they repulsed me.

Gun saw this – he turned to me and spoke loudly, I assumed so that they could hear, "You are Mark's woman. You will stay with him. Kiowa will watch over you until Mark comes."

Seeming to feel caught, one of the men backed away, the tentacle-like penis of his imagination receding from deep inside me. The other men followed suit, took their invisible mental paws off me, pulled their minds out of my private parts, and took their teeth out of my flesh. I could feel myself being released – soiled by their thoughts but released.

"Mark's gone on a sighting hike 'til the next night," the first man said.

"And Kiowa?" Gun asked.

"Kiowa will come tonight."

"I will stay at least until then," Gun said sternly, as if issuing the men a warning. I issued myself a warning too: watch out – watch your back. So far, only Gun seemed safe. And why wasn't Mark here? Something was wrong, something had to be wrong for Mark not to greet me. He and I were so close – born the same year, he just two days older. We looked so similar that we had often been mistaken for brother and sister – we had the same skin, eye and hair coloring. We

64

actually felt like brother and sister. Our relationship was innocent, and our love was naïve.

"Show me where Mark sleeps," Gun directed one of the men, a heavy set one who had been toying with his gun.

That man turned his eyes onto me, and a wave of crazed Fire Star energy again hit me. "Okay, yeah," was all that he answered as he turned to lumber across the field and show us the way.

"Come on, grab your things," Gun said to me. "I cannot carry them for you; these men would not honor me if I did. And we both need them to honor me right now. Mainly you do."

"I can carry my stuff myself anyway." I sounded matter of fact. I was trying to decide what to do next. I didn't like this place. Should I stay and wait for Mark? Why wasn't he here to greet me? Surely he didn't want to leave me alone with these people. Overwhelmed by a strange despair-laden fatigue, I followed Gun reluctantly, dragging my pack behind me, feeling that I was being led behind what now seemed to be enemy lines.

Gun was talking as we hiked. "We hope to teach the men of the Tribe new ways. But they have already learned too well the old ways of seeing the outside world, and of how to treat people who come from the outside."

Suddenly I was very mad. A river of anger welled up inside me. I surprised myself with my sudden outburst. "Pretty disgusting if you ask me. I hate the way they look at women. White women anyway."

Gun stopped walking and whirled around to face me. He remained calm however. "Well, so now you know exactly how they and their land and their women and their daughters have been treated by many a white man for centuries."

But Gun's explanation didn't calm me. "But I'm not white *man*. And I'm only partly white. Can't they tell?"

"But maybe you are just like many white people who think they are not white. There will be more like you as the coming Earth changes, and economic shifts, begin to threaten the survival of the white race. Whites will see the knowledge we people have carried through time. Finally they will value it … and try to steal it from us. Or they will try to copy it. Or they will try to join us for it. They think they can be Native American just by wanting to be." Gun chuckled, "Some kind of hi-tech wish magic." And then he became somber again. "But it doesn't work that way. A true blending of people is key to everyone's survival."

Now Gun walked on a few yards, waved off the man who had been leading the way, and stopped in the doorway of an old building. "Put your things in here. This barn is where Mark sleeps." I did what Gun had suggested and dropped my pack in the doorway. "Good," he said, "now, let's go over the mountain to the circle. They'll be gathering there soon. Everyone is fasting for at least three days."

"Not me. I already haven't eaten in days; I don't even know how many. At least two. No three. Maybe four. I'm famished. I need food now."

"Good. This is at least your third day then. The hunger will pass soon. There is no food up here right now, anyway. Just tea. Drink it. The tea helps a lot. You'll be okay. And maybe you will even become *wakan*."

I would become *wakan*? *Wakan*? What was that? The word had caught my ear, but I had other more important concerns. I was resolute and surprisingly firm now. "Gun, I'll just leave with you when you go."

He smiled just a bit and very softly. "I cannot take you where I am going. It's deeper into the mountains to meet Creator for some visions. A quest. I'll be leaving my truck at the foot of a very rough trail. Anyway, I won't be gone long. I'll be back around the time of the naming ceremony."

Naming ceremony? Strange notion, I said to myself, ceremony for naming what? "Well then, I'll stay and leave with Mark. Mark'll get me out of here."

Gun looked at me and shook his head gently. "Well, don't hold your breath. There aren't many rides out. Why don't you just not make any plans? Wait and see. See what you can learn here. It's actually real good stuff. *You know, old wisdom does not always come to you in shiny gift wrap tied with pretty ribbon*."

He looked me in the eye kindly but solemnly, then took my left hand, which was clenched, opened it, and squeezed it flat between his palms. He smiled but was serious. "It's time for you to meet the spirits we people know. You will see you have come here for more than

Mark. This journey has been made by you for you and for your people. And maybe even for our people."

Gun paused, studying my face closely, as if he was seeing me for the first time. He took a deep breath. "Oh my," was all he said, "oh my great Creator."

I pulled my hand out from between his palms and looked at him with raised eyebrows. "I'm out'a here, soon as possible."

Taken aback by something, I didn't know what, Gun folded his arms loosely, started to close his eyes, and then abruptly opened his eyes wide and looked up into the sky as if he saw something there. Seeming to hear sound from somewhere invisible, he nodded and then asked me, "Do you know the story of the white buffalo?"

I shook my head no. And I don't want to know, I told myself. But this man, Gun, was being kind to me, and I needed this.

Gun closed his eyes and went on, "You should know this story now. You are white, but of mixed blood, I see this. So, long ago, during a time of great famine, a woman came wearing buffalo – *tatanka* – skin and carrying a pipe. She taught the people how to use the pipe in ceremony, how to connect the Earth and sky. She showed how blessings could be brought by the pipe. Those people did pipe ceremony ever since and did not have famine again." Gun opened one eye to see if I was listening.

I was definitely disinterested, and I made sure my face showed this. Yet, for some reason, my mind was picturing the story Gun was telling as if I was being shown a child's picture book.

Gun opened both eyes and faced me squarely. "She taught the people many things and then left, saying she would return when time called her back. She would return when it was *the* time."

Gun looked at me to be sure he had my attention. I rolled my eyes. He raised his voice a little. "She left, heading into the west." Gun faced west.

I rolled my eyes.

"As she left, her body rolled and turned into a black buffalo." Gun whirled his arm in a circle. "Then it rolled again, and ..." Gun said as he stood tall. He looked at me. I rolled my eyes. He suddenly did a sort of somersault. This got my attention, but I concealed my shift in interest as best I could.

"... and turned into a brown buffalo." Gun looked at me for a sign of interest. I gave him no sign.

"Then ..." he said as he did another somersault, "... it rolled again and turned into a red buffalo. Then it rolled again," he said with another somersault, "and turned into a young white female buffalo and disappeared."

Now I could see, in the distance of my imagination, this strange image of a woman rolling and becoming a buffalo that changed colors until she was a white one. Did white buffalo exist, I wondered. And then I caught myself being a bit interested and shut my interest off right away. I scowled and heaved a bored sigh. "So, what's your point?" I asked.

"People waited a long time for her return and looked always for the birth of white buffaloes – actually one birth made up of four – four white buffaloes, one for each of the four directions."

"Big deal," I muttered.

Gun sat down abruptly and patted the ground, expecting me to sit. I didn't move. He got back up on his feet and gently took hold of my shoulders. "Listen up, young lady, some of us have had visions of the next white buffalo coming … yes, female, coming from the west, heralding the new time, the Earth change time, delivering it in …."

He looked at me intensely. I was blank. What he was saying meant nothing to me. Still he continued, "The return of the white buffalo, especially the fourth one, is something like the second coming of Christ is to Christians, you know."

"No, I don't know," I said dully.

Gun squinted into my eyes, as if I knew something I wasn't saying. "But it seems something more is going on with this."

I really couldn't relate to what he was saying, and I really didn't care about it. I shrugged nonchalantly.

"Hmmm," he said, "the time is coming for the removal of ignorance. Then we will see. Spirit will tell us. I think you will see, too."

He waited to see what I would do with this information – but I felt numb, I didn't react. I stared at the ground. Right then, I didn't care about any myths or visions. Not anymore. I just wanted out.

Gun was unfazed by my lack of interest. He added, "We are not certain what Fire Star thinks about you. He is not saying. Some of the elders say he has taken you for his own. But it does not really matter. There were signs predicting your arrival here, just the way it has happened. And there have been visions telling us …."

Gun stopped and watched me angrily cover up my sudden curiosity with a blank nonplused stare. He seemed to decide not to tell me something else and then said gently, "Look, we will let it be for now. The time will come when you will know who you are better than anyone else does. You went through a lot to get here. You spent the time of your whole young life so far heading this way. It's pretty obvious you have a job to do. So you should do the job. Do the journey."

Do the journey? I didn't really know what he meant. And I was faintly suspicious. Why would anyone let Fire Star treat a girl they thought of as special the way he had treated me?

Still, I could see that Gun thought what he was saying was very important. He seemed to be a good man. I could see his intelligence and deep spirit. I wanted to trust my instincts. He did not feel like Fire Star. But then Gun was not doing to my mind and body what Fire Star had done. Not doing it right now, I warned myself. I wondered how I could trust my instincts in a situation so radically different from any I was used to. Or anything I thought I was used to.

Gun had gone on talking and I had missed what he had said. He saw that I wasn't listening at all. "So let's get on with it," he nudged.

"Get on with what?" I said with muffled irritation.

I wasn't in a good mood. I was fiercely upset about my predicament and seeming powerlessness, and I was very tired and very hungry. The hunger and exhaustion is how I tried to explain to myself what happened next. In that moment, Fire Star's face appeared in great detail, floating in the air before me. Startled, I rubbed my eyes hard and forced several blinks, but he didn't go away.

"Get on with the journey," Gun said, unaware of what I was seeing, his enduring patience evident in the tone of his voice. He stood, started walking off, and beckoned me to follow.

Some journey, I thought to myself. I wasn't really there for it, wasn't really on it, or was I? I didn't feel very present. Still, I followed Gun, stumbling along in his footsteps, trying not to see Fire Star's haunting face, staring at the ground to be sure I was touching Earth. There I was, embarking on this thing Gun called the journey, even though, with each new step, I found myself feeling that I was already dead, not really alive in this body that was moving me over this rough trail.

"Stay close, don't get lost," Gun advised from up ahead.

Lost.

6.
somehow dead

But lost was part of the journey.

As I followed Gun onto a steep trail, I kept seeing Fire Star's face staring me in the eye. He took on a nagging sort of reality, his essence seeming far too present to be merely my imagination. I clenched my teeth. Fire Star was stalking my psyche. He can actually do this, I warned myself. Was this going to lead to some kind of showdown? Could I ever win it? I told myself I was at a distinct disadvantage, especially if I had been somehow dead since this Fire Star had strangled me.

This was a confusing predicament. I remembered dying. I had experienced being killed – strangled – by Fire Star. But here I was, my body still intact – walking, talking, breathing, seeing, being. My body was alive, following Gun to some apparently sacred place. Yet I felt dead – tired to the core, wasted, consumed, gone.

And Fire Star's face, it continued to loom before me in some vague ethereal dimension as I walked on. It was switching back and forth – pulsating between a human and a Fire Star-like version of the same man.

I walked on, stumbling a lot. I chastised myself for the miserable failure of my instincts. Fire Star had taken me because I'd been there for the taking – my instincts had brought me to him. My instincts should have kept me out of that building and out of that somehow proclaimed medicine man's reach. Instead, I'd walked right into his game, and he had hurt not only my body; he had hurt my soul. I wanted to take a knife and cut the memory of his violation out of my flesh. But how would I ever exorcise my soul of his intrusion, of his grizzly attack on my spirit?

"Just a little further to go; the clearing is up ahead," Gun noted from in front of me.

I continued following Gun, but my body continued feeling more and more strange, further and further from me. This sensation made me nervous. Obviously, I was still connected to my flesh, I could feel and even see the tie to it, but I was also becoming ever more aware by the moment that I was floating above my body, rather than living within it. That body I had once called "me" now seemed merely a container, a vessel, for the me somehow acting from above it, to make it walk and talk and function.

With a massive jolt, I realized with absolute clarity that that body of mine down there on the Earth, the body I saw walking along, was a living vessel for me to inhabit – but – but what? I was also a vessel for more – yes, for more – more than just my self! This sudden conceptual dawning was so overwhelming that I would have leapt out of my skin in shock, if my consciousness hadn't already been literally out of my skin.

I impulsively lurched, from a point already outside my body, to a point higher upward, further away from my body – further into the sky – upward until I hit some kind of invisible ceiling where I hit my head hard. At the same time, I heard my body gasp down below me, and looking down, saw its hand go to rub the top of its head where it felt it had been hit.

My awareness fell downward suddenly toward the ground – crashing down and hitting something I couldn't see, some kind of invisible floor. My consciousness landed hard a few feet above my body – and my body fell to the ground.

Gun turned around quickly. "Are you still with me?"

I couldn't speak. I made my body nod a yes.

"Are you hurt?"

I made my body nod a no.

"Can you stand up?"

I made my body nod a yes and stand up on the path.

"Come on then, the gathering is right over this rise. The ceremony is beginning. You will soon discover the importance of this hike." Gun walked on, leading the way again. I was unable to muster up any defiance and I followed silently. I made my body walk on into my journey, and I, being attached to that body, went with it.

Stumbling down the trail toward some ceremony, I became overwhelmed by this nagging sensation, the perception, that I was not alone in that body – that I had company. It's like being alone in a dark room and suddenly realizing there are others in there with you. Those Seven ancient beings – priestesses it seemed – who had saved my life in the midst of Fire Star's raping me, were here in this consciousness of mine. They were also corded to what I considered my flesh – corded through my consciousness to my body – even when I was outside my body.

Suddenly there they were, gathered all around me, right where Fire Star's face had loomed moments before. Seven luminous bluish white beings surrounding me, as clear as day! And they were so, so beautiful, with a loving energy, a loving light emanating from their inner presences and washing through and through me.

Every piece of my being started to cry, my tears becoming a shrine to the unsurpassable magnificence of these light beings. And I surrendered without hesitation to the realization that the body I had thought was mine alone was, in truth, the physical embodiment being shared by several other related minds, a team of what seemed to be female consciousnesses who were using my body to do their Work. "Oh, yes!" I found myself saying, "Oh yes!"

"You, and others like you, have known this all along," I heard their Seven glorious voices tell me in unison.

"I have? We have?" I wondered. But yes, somehow this did indeed all seem obvious to me. I didn't exactly know others like me, like whatever I was, but I was rather glad there were others like me out there. Were we all having to come into this awareness via such troubled pathways? I did not know, but I could feel there were others on this path I was following.

The obviousness of the larger realization here, that I had somehow known all this all along, made it all the more rattling. I actually had somehow already known that I was something far more expansive than one person in that youthful human girl's body.

Still, at the same time, part of me wanted to tell myself that all this was just an illusion being had by a hurting and hungry body, and a lost and lonely girl. I wanted to know I could regain a normal perception of the world, or at least what I had thought was normal before all this.

They spoke more to me: "That body you call yours has been our address for a while and it will be for many years more, but it has never been home. You operate the vessel of this flesh you call your own from outside it, along with us. Your persona is designed to be mostly amnesic and somewhat naive – considering your extra-dimensional origins. You were formed by we Seven spirits to be the persona using this body, to return to and live in this world at this time – to be our working arm here. You are us. We are here to bring on the Great Return, and to guide its process for the good of all."

The Great Return! A magnificent rush of awareness streamed through me. I shivered intensely and shook uncontrollably as they embraced my soul. I wanted to dissolve in this unworldly bliss. Why go on in the third dimension, the material plane, when this ecstasy awaits just beyond it, I asked myself.

But right then, I felt a jolt run from the Earth up through the bottoms of my feet and into my body. Startled, I told myself that I couldn't afford to dwell on these outrageous realizations any longer.

My physical survival could still be at stake: far too many tidal waves of physical plane experience were washing through me for me to continue reflecting on this dangerously transfixing joint occupation of my flesh.

I popped harshly back into somewhat more normal consciousness and saw that Gun and I had completed our hike. We were walking into a strange clearing, way out in the middle of nowhere, deep in the woods. We were outdoors, but it felt distinctly like we were in a wall-less room – a way-station where people gathered to catch a ride somewhere – a portal to another reality I sensed.

I wanted to dislike what I'd found but I just couldn't. It seemed to me that I had somehow entered an outdoor temple honoring the Earth, and through Earth, honoring all Creation. This was a strange, strange place. We could have been in a bubble floating in space, everything was so very unearthly. A sense of the sacred surrounded me. My hunger for food faded as I realized that I had been starving for this experience of the sacred for eons. Is this why I came here?

I became aware that Gun and I had followed a dull, sensuously throbbing drumbeat to this special place. And now we were surrounded by – enmeshed in – that beat. We were also surrounded by perhaps fifty, even more, people. I was dazzled by the dress of the people collected there. Some wore just leather loincloths, others wore beaded vests and colorfully painted gowns or long shirts, with things sewn onto them, hanging out over ragged blue jeans. Most had feathers and sticks in their hair and ears and around their necks and wrists and ankles. Many of their faces were painted. Some of their arms and chests were painted as well.

"Come let us paint you." An older woman grabbed me.

"No, not right now," Gun told her. He led me off. "It's just a new tradition built on the old – they are trying to mix the old together and add some, like a giant stew, I guess," he explained, chuckling. "But seriously, they are merging traditions here, to save the best of the best of them. Sit with me and we will have some tea."

Gun took me away from the center of that hot-spot, over to the edge of the clearing. I sat on a large tree stump with Gun, just being there at what seemed to be the front entrance or staging area of the clearing. I watched the festivities. Drumming and dancing seemed to be erupting all around us.

People seemed to revere Gun. Many of them came to him and offered him puffs on long, engraved pipes, muttering something about "*Wakan Tanka,*" whatever that was, I said to myself. I couldn't help but wonder what all this was about. Gun must have heard me wondering. In the middle of the process, he leaned over to me and whispered, "*Wakan Tanka* is the great mystery, the mystery of creation and Creator. Well, it was the Lakota Sioux term for Creator, but now many call him *Wakan Tanka.*"

He was handed another pipe. He took a puff after aiming the pipe in four directions. Then he held the pipe near me and turned it in four directions. Then he offered me a puff. I put my mouth on it but didn't inhale.

Gun again turned the pipe in four directions. I realized now that these directions were north, west, south, east. "Offerings are made to the Creator with these pipes," he said, "the way the white buffalo woman taught people to do." Gun stared at me as if I knew all this.

A woman with long gray braids and a beaded leather gown brought Gun and me mugs of tea. She thrust one of the mugs into my hands.

"Drink," said Gun.

I was real thirsty. I took a sip and then hesitated. "What's this stuff?"

"Peyote. Or as our friends the Huichol Indians of Mexico call it, *hikuli* – tea. Corn for the soul. Made from sacred cactus."

I tried to hand him my cup.

"Do not worry about it. It is so mild. And it is all there is to drink or eat this week. Keeps you going." He saw me look at the contents of the cup with distrust. "It is okay, really. It is just a ceremonial tea. Many tribes have used it for many thousands of years. Souls cross, healings happen. But the feelings from the tea are gentle."

"Look, I'm just thirsty. I need water, that's all," I said quietly.

"You can quench your thirst long before you get any really big effect. Then, if you want to go for more, you can decide later to keep drinking. If you do decide, do not worry about your stomach. You do not really get sick when you take it as tea. Not really."

My thirst overwhelmed me. I took a couple more sips. I was relieved to discover that the tea had no effect on me. I drank yet a few more sips. It had been sweetened a lot, I figured with honey.

People seemed to be lining up to say hello to Gun. I moved off of the stump and stood awkwardly to his side, facing away from the line. I felt shy and out of place. Most of the people there were Americans – Native Americans. I thought I looked very white before them all, even with my olive-toned skin. I felt very white, and very dirty.

A woman came over to me. "Hi. I am Running Horse Woman. I live at the other camp. I do the girl's painting."

"Hi." I didn't know what to say.

"You getting named this week?"

"No."

"Oh?" the woman sounded surprised at my answer. She seemed to want to continue the conversation. "You do know Fire Star, the big chief, don't you?"

I shut my eyes. "Yeah." I opened my eyes and scowled.

She looked at me knowingly. "Ever done this before?"

"No, and I'm not part of this."

She looked a little perturbed, and I couldn't quite figure out why. But she was still nice to me. "Well, maybe you don't know it's a privilege to be allowed to participate if you are not one of us. They call your name out of the east, south, west and north. Then a vision comes and that is what you are. Spirit names you. It's who you really are. This is how my Cherokee grandfather named me."

I rolled my eyes with gentle disdain.

She was patient. "Don't you know anything about this ... about why you're up here? About how important it is that you're here?"

"No, I just got here ... I'm just waiting for Mark."

She backed off the topic. "Oh, right, you're Mark's girl. I met him. Nice boy."

I didn't have more to say so I looked back at my mug and drank the rest of my tea. Someone appeared from behind me and filled my mug to the brim again. I drank that too without thinking about it.

The afternoon continued with drumming and dancing. Step by step, the day transformed itself, by the unrecognized magic of everyday nature, into a sublime dusk. The light of the departing sun became a glow filtering through the forest-lined horizon. Everyone looked like a Native American now, all their faces bronzed in the sunset, at least to me. And I found that I felt like one, too. In fact it seemed I really was one. But then, at least part of me was one, at least by blood.... My sense of being an outsider, of my separateness, began to diminish.

More people gathered around what was once a solo drummer. The beat had become louder, deeper and more resonant. I could practically see the music, it was coming so alive. Some people had been dancing for hours. I started seeing violet halos around them. I thought my eyes were becoming tired from watching them so long. A lot of what they were calling "medicine weed" was being circulated. Huge cauldrons full of more of that ceremonial tea were heating around the perimeter of a large fire in a deep pit.

I experienced the distinct perception of being in a huge fish bowl, with the fire at the bottom of it and everyone dancing and swimming around the glass sides. Everyone could see everything. Everyone could see me. I could see everyone, what they really looked like. I could see their long shadows following them, bending on the sides of the glass bowl. Some shadows were changing colors, as if the setting sun and the dancing firelight were changing their temperatures or something, I didn't know.

I still sat mostly alone.

Then a new person appeared in my visual field.

7.
rushing water

"I, I am Kiowa, I just came in…."

Kiowa paused a moment and looked me in the eye. Then he went on, "I am your guide. An unofficial *wa-na-nee-che*."

Kiowa, the magnificent, blue-eyed, red man as he proudly called himself, wearing a leather headband, a little white leather bag around his neck, faded jeans, no shirt, a leather vest, and old moccasins, stood before me. I blinked, trying to separate him from his brilliant blue shadow. I stood up from the tree stump where I had been sitting for quite some time. How long, I wondered.

As I stood, I reeled with a wave of nausea and dizziness. Kiowa's strong arm reached across my back. I blinked and shook my head, as if to shake the fog out of it.

"Wow, I'm dizzy I guess."

"Must be the tea."

"I guess so."

"I am here to protect your spirit, to guide your spirit across the divide," he announced calmly. "A spiritual advisor or *wa-na-nee-che* sometimes does this."

I blurted out, "Does this mean I am dead?"

Kiowa stared right into my soul with his blue flame eyes – a flame which all of a sudden was strikingly familiar to me: In the instant I saw the flame, I realized I had seen it living in my father's eyes, too. Kiowa saw me know this, nodded a yes. I could see he knew that I was dead. Was Kiowa dead, too?

"Die? What does that mean?" he said.

I had no answer. After all, die means nothing, absolutely nothing and everything all at once. That's to die, I told myself. I looked up at the sky and it seemed to swoosh down and envelope me. I gulped in too much air and choked.

Kiowa looked at me with slight concern. "You all right?"

I nodded a yes.

He grinned. "Sometimes the truth is a lot to swallow."

"I think I'm a bit scared. Is this safe? I mean, I drank a lot of that tea."

"Yes, it is safe, but people who are not carefully trained should always have a guide. White people – well actually even red people who are living in the white world – even people of every color – modern people – they forget that this material is for ceremony, not recreation. You are drinking strong medicine. You move to the *wakan* state, the state of spiritual openness. That way you can enter other worlds. This must be done with great care and great respect."

I raised my eyebrows, a bit curious.

"You are moving to the *wakan* now. So that is what I am, your guide."

Kiowa helped me sit back down on the tree stump, guiding me by the shoulders. "But I don't know you," I said. "Are you with those men with guns I saw today?"

"No, I certainly am not. They are still learning the way."

"I don't like their shadows," I found myself saying without forethought.

"No one will harm you."

"You have a good shadow," I told Kiowa.

"I am a harmless guide in the woods, in the spirit realm, the land beyond ... the wilderness of the heart."

My attention shifted. I was watching a line of people dancing through the bowl. Most of the dancers had removed most of their clothes. The thought hit me – were they dead, too? Stripped of their Earth lives?

"It is my job to guide you through the coming days. You are, you know, crying for a vision."

"Not that I know of." I wasn't quite following him.

"Moving into adulthood, a person asks, who am I? Why am I here? I like the Lakota name for the ritual where the young adult cries for this vision of his or her life and place in the universe: *hanblechaya*. It is a rite-of-passage."

"Uh huh." I was moving my head in time with the hypnotic drum beat, very slowly. I was staring at the fire.

"We can take a walk now."

"I'm waiting for Mark."

"He decided not to come to you until the naming ceremony. So, let us use your time well. There is much to be learned, to prepare."

Kiowa took me by the hand and gently led me to the edge of the fishbowl. There I stopped, rigid and refusing to move. "I can't go there, it's very dark, all shadow, like a black soup."

"I am your eyes until the dark becomes the light … I will guide you now … it will be okay."

"O – kaaaayyyy." I swallowed what I told myself was my silly fear. "Let's try just a little way out."

Kiowa took me by the hand and led me to a path winding into the forest. It looked like a river into blackness. The moon had not come up yet. We walked out. I stumbled several times, and Kiowa caught me before I hit the ground each time.

"What's that talking sound?" I stopped in my tracks and resisted Kiowa's forward pull on my hand.

Kiowa stopped and was quiet for a while. "That is the river. Water talking. It is good that you can hear it from so far off."

"Let's go there and see what it's saying." I was suddenly eager for Kiowa's guidance. I reached for his hand, making a motion saying that I would indeed follow.

Kiowa withdrew his hand and did not move ahead. He pushed me to lead. "See if you can find the river."

"But it's dark. I can't see."

"Then close your eyes."

I did so, wondering why I would do such a thing.

"Now keep your eyes closed until later when I tell you to open them." Kiowa turned and faced me. He put his hands on my head. "I will give you old ways of being with the trees and the rocks, old ways of being in the night. You will have these old ways to use for the rest of your life. You will have them to use and to teach. You will be very careful about who you choose to teach these old ways to. They are the ways of my ancestor families and the many star families before them."

He placed one forefinger on top of each of my eyelids. "Keep your eyelids closed." Then his two hands moved as if to cover my two ears. He held his hands a few inches away from my head, as if to amplify something. "Now, listen and follow the sound."

"What if I fall?"

"You must be very slow, almost as slow as frozen water. You can let go of fear; you are safe with me. I will protect you from all falls, all dangers. Sometime soon, you will learn to protect yourself. Danger is only a reflection of how you choose to be in the world. Now listen to your feet … stay close to the ground … be part of the ground, the Earth … walk gently on the land … only small, very quiet, soft steps … listen to the shape of the place where you are … be in it with care … keep your eyes closed … feel the stillness move."

I absorbed these directions. Their knowledge became part of me. I moved the way I imagined Kiowa meant for me to do. Time stretched out to a plateau of forever. I became more still than still, moving all the while. It seemed that I hardly moved at all.

"Now keep your eyes closed and say her name," Kiowa instructed in a soft voice.

I whispered back, "Don't understand what you mean."

"She will take you there. Say her name if you want to travel on her energy."

"Name?"

"River, river, river," Kiowa whispered.

"River, river, river," I chanted quietly.

The river seemed to just come to me. I could hear it get closer. I said something I really didn't understand under my breath: "Like rushing water, nothing moves."

"Exactly," Kiowa said. "Now open your eyes."

I did so and gasped. "Rushing water," I whispered in awe. Now, the rising moonlight was dancing like milk flowing from the sky and splashing onto the water. The surfaces of the moonlight and the river water were undulating in a love dance. I could not tell where the river ended and my body began. "I got here by magic?"

"Well, not really. You traveled on the rushing of the water."

"Magic. A magic carpet ride," I marveled.

Kiowa smiled. "Well, you can call it that. But true magic is expertise. What happened is that you moved through space and time by saying her name."

"Whose name?"

"River's name. The goddess of rushing water. The opening comes when you say her name."

"That's amazing." I moved into the water.

I turned to Kiowa. "Oh, I get it now. '*Sayeth my name if thou wouldst travel upon me.*' "

Kiowa looked a little surprised. "Sounds about right. But where have you heard this before, said like that?"

"My mother. My mother used to read it to me from an old book when I was a little girl."

I saw the water rushing around me. Still no edge between my flesh and the flow. I became the rushing water. I could feel Kiowa's guiding arm still on me, but at the point where he touched me, we too seemed to merge, no edge between us.

"So always remember to say her name."

"What?" I murmured as I touched the surface of the water with my fingertips.

"Say her name when you choose to travel upon her."

"I will, I promise." I wanted to thank Kiowa for showing me this special way. I turned and saw his blue, blue eyes shining in the night light. He seemed to be so entirely aware of me that there were no boundaries between even our minds. "So you are me, too," I said.

He looked into my eyes and touched my forehead. "Perhaps this is the real reason you have come here, to be closer to the Mother Earth, the great Maka, for the great Maka Shan."

"My mother is with the Earth. My mother is dead. I guess she is with all the Earths and all the Stars out there." I waved at the star-filled sky. It felt like I was stirring a soup. "So are we. With all the Earths and Stars." I felt so close to my mother now, and to the Earth.

Kiowa nodded.

I felt I could tell him something very private. "Kiowa, I'm not from here – not from this time or this place or even this planet. I know

now more than ever – I've been here before – this Earth, but I come, somehow – from the stars."

Kiowa nodded and said simply: "So do I."

"Kiowa, I seem to have voices within me. Old women from way out there." I pointed at the sky.

Kiowa studied me and then nodded gravely. "I can see that."

I felt the most intense yearning overwhelm me. "Kiowa, I want to go home." I pointed at the sky.

"I know you do," he said. "And you will eventually learn to come and go from here to home more easily. It's the kind of thing spirits like us forget when we are born here."

"But I want to go there now."

Kiowa chuckled softly. "Your time will come. First, your visions must teach you to find your way and to do your Work. You have sacrificed a great deal to be here, I am sure."

I felt the pressure of my own culture heavy on my chest just then. "People I grew up with, my friends," I said, "they didn't ever let me talk this way – so I hid it and sometimes my memory of home faded."

"In my family, this was the only way we talked," he answered. "It was just part of life, that we are not from this place. Our sacred history always told us of our ancestors, and of our star knowledge. This is our heritage."

Kiowa unexpectedly laughed like a child, then grew silent – and his eyes filled with happiness as he went on. "I learned as a child, from my grandmother, how I had come here to care for this Earth, our new mother, and that some of us were to travel back and forth – from Earth to stars and back – with the ancestors who came to visit. I was trained early to know I was a wanderer and a guide for wanderers. I was one to come and go."

"You know, Kiowa, my parents actually understood me – they said they knew what I was talking about when I told them I didn't feel like I came from here. But they warned me that other people wouldn't understand."

"They were right. The white world cannot see this. The white world has tried to kill our teachings, to stop the star knowledge … to close the doorway to the spirit realm."

He gazed up into the sky. "We have an old story about going to the stars. I must have heard it thousands of times when I was a boy. Every time I loved hearing it. Should I tell it to you?"

"Well, sure."

"Okay, it went like this: Seven young sisters, who were spending their lives preparing for a ceremony that they did not yet understand, and one boy, who thought he would someday be a great medicine man, were playing together. The boy was pretending to be a bear. He was pretending very hard. Then, all of a sudden, he became a real dangerous, hungry, growling and roaring bear with real fur and claws. The girls ran off, very terrified. The wild bear chased after them. The Seven girls were in great danger until they heard a voice coming out of the ground that called them to a tree stump and told them to climb onto the stump for safety. This made no sense to them but they did it. And then the tree stump grew taller and taller until it was reaching deep into the sky. These girls stayed there. You still see them out there today. They are the Seven Pleiades stars."

He pointed at the Pleiadean constellation. And then he pointed my hand that way, too. I could almost see the Seven Sisters there, as if their faces were forming in the sky. "Oh, they're beautiful." They looked a little familiar.

"People thought the bear had killed the sisters and eaten them, but the girls had found the doorway home. The bear had been their means of transport – of sacrifice. The Earth showed them the way, directing them to ride the tree stump home through the doorway to the sky world."

Kiowa's story brought back vague, elusive, memories of something that I couldn't quite bring into focus. I didn't yet get its connection to my life. Words familiar to me ever since my childhood came to my mind. "Mother Earth, take me. Send me home," I murmured.

Kiowa looked pleasantly surprised. "How do you know that prayer?" he asked me.

"It's a prayer? Ummm, I just say it to myself once in a while … and your story made me think of it."

"Hmmmm." Kiowa touched my hand with his. Then he touched my forehead. Then he touched my heart. "*Aho, Mitakuye Oyasin*. All my relations, all are related."

I repeated his words, "*Mitakuye Oyasin….*"

Kiowa seemed to like that I had done so. He patted me on the head and continued, "My grandmother often told me how our people came here from those stars where the sisters went," he said, pointing. "You see, the Seven Sisters just went home again, to their kingdom, to prepare for their next visit to this place – for the Great Return of the priestess power – the great rebalancing to come."

This story made me so wistful that I overlooked Kiowa's note about the Great Return and consequent rebalancing to come. I sighed, tears coming to my eyes. "This is such a long way to be from home."

"It is only as far as you make it."

"Do you go there, Kiowa?" I pointed there, again at his Seven stars.

He paused. "Sometimes. In ceremony. Once not in ceremony … at least not my people's ceremony. That time, I was in the trenches … where men were dying."

"Trenches?" I asked. "What trenches?"

"Nam."

"Nam? What's that?" I still didn't get it.

"Viet—"

Then I got it. "Viet Nam? You were there?"

"Red man canon fodder, point men, front line warriors. Even Green Beret. Red warriors, dying for the U.S. of A. … For what though…." With that, Kiowa folded his knees close in to his chest and rocked for just a moment, as if drifting off.

And suddenly the air opened up right in front of us, and I experienced both of us going through the hole in the air – right into the trenches. I could see Kiowa's memory, almost touch it. What a massacre!

Men dying everywhere. Their blood running into the Viet Namese Earth, a land of ancient spirits. All around us, souls leaving flesh, and then hovering, wanting help, wanting ceremony, wanting prayer. Kiowa wanting, needing, to perform rituals for their passage, right there under the bullets and bombs. Sacred caring, prayer, being denied. Kiowa fighting for the right to protect these souls in a foreign land we had invaded, Viet Nam, that had actually, for tens of thousands of years, practiced its own rituals for the protection of the souls of the dead. Kiowa not understanding white war, white rules. White reasons in the heart of the chaos with no heart. I could see Kiowa seeing the Viet Namese blood mixing with Native American blood mixing with white blood and black blood and more blood and more blood. But the blood itself was all the same color....

I was very scared, this seemed too real, as if the war – the blood -- and even the souls of the dead -- had suddenly jumped to the space around me. I was right there with him: blood and bombs and screams of men in the air. I could feel his misery – feel the death around him – feel him being denied the rituals for the dying and dead that he was so bound to practice by his faith. My heart started to pound almost out of my chest. I moved to leap up, hoping to escape either the trench or my skin.

Kiowa put his hand on my knee forcefully, to stop me, looked me right in the eye a moment, then started humming a quiet, slow chant. He ritually made gestures in the four directions, north east south west. Then he took some river water and splashed it over my head, making me gasp.

"What are you doing?" I whispered.

"Closing the opening. I am sorry, your guide got lost for a time. I should not have taken you there. Or maybe it was meant to be that I did. But, we must always be careful what visions we visit when in spirit realm. Visions become real. This is good for working in them, for healing time, but not for training you right now." He waved his arm. "All will be well."

And it was. The pictures were gone. The problems were gone. It would be long into my own future before I would understand what I had learned about the passage of the dying into the spirit realm, and about my own commitment to helping with this practice – and what this had to do with the Work the Seven reminded me I had come to do.

In the mean time, the sublime soup of stars and night sky floated back in.

8.
night sky

The fast continued.

Time danced on, leading its own life, as if it were a separate spirit with its own will. Another turn of the sun, a night and a day, went by. I continued drinking the tea, accepting the medicine weed when it came to me now, completely forgetting that I had not eaten since before I arrived at the house in Sacramento.

"Are you ready? Let us paint you for the ceremony, young priestess." Three women with painted faces began to take my shirt off. Now I did not resist. I didn't know why. Perhaps I had no energy for resistance. Perhaps I was now willing to be part of it all. This kind of experience can be so intense that what a person had wanted out of life, what a person had believed about life, who a person thought she or he was, can just dissolve away.

They painted my naked breasts as if each one were the center of a sun, with Seven rays coming off of each center. They tied feathers in my long two-braided hair with thin strips of leather. One of the women put her own beaded headband around my head. Another removed several of her silver bracelets and put them onto my wrists. "Let me take off your old jeans. We can paint your legs, too. I have a piece of leather to tie around your hips."

They removed my jeans. I didn't have much opinion about what was happening. It was just happening. I felt like a princess being adorned, but also like a corpse being dressed for her casket. I heard the women talking about a ceremony. I said nothing. I just yawned. Another day had flowed over the edge of the Earth, pursued by the first fingers of a sensuous night.

More tea.

There was new activity at the far corner of the fish bowl. A large procession of what looked like one or two hundred people was arriving. They filled the bowl space with their bodies, like a liquid made of people. The liquid gave off many lights. One light was very big and dark like a threatening magnet. I was concerned. I jerked and pulled away from the women who had finished tying the leather around my hips but who were still painting my legs. I had to get far away from that dark and magnetic light. I turned to run out of the bowl.

I found that my legs could not carry me except in slow motion. Blindly, I moved straight into Kiowa, who stood gently in my way. "Where are you going without your guide?"

For a moment, I distrusted Kiowa and eyed him as if he were a dangerous animal about to spring upon me from a boulder in the mountains. Then I remembered and focused on his brilliant blue shadow and my identity with him.

I was shaking all over. Kiowa narrowed his eyes and studied my face, then looked across the clearing and saw that Fire Star, the chief, had just arrived. Kiowa held me by the shoulders and closed his eyes for a moment. When he opened his eyes, they were filled with tears. "Oh, I understand now, what has happened to you. This will not happen again. Try to hear me."

I was shaking into convulsions. I was seeing Fire Star as he really was. I was overwhelmed by this vision, and the memory of my visit to his bed throne. Kiowa had to work to get my attention. He spoke caringly but loudly and sharply, right into my soul. I began to try to hear him. "Look at me. You are safe. You will not be violated here. He will not take you here. There are too many braves who would want you for their own. He would not compete with them."

But this information didn't exactly make me feel any better. I started to shake harder. Kiowa put his hand on my forehead. "Fire Star cannot really win such a fight."

I cringed. Kiowa realized that he was making a mistake – that I was not feeling better – that he was telling me without meaning to that I might find myself prey in an animal hunt, with all these men here as competing hunters, acting like animals, hungry bears. Could it be that this dynamic was possible in our times? Yes.

It might have been the truth had Kiowa not been there. But, he tried again. "What I am saying is that you are all right here. You are with me. You are protected by me. No one will touch you or hurt you now. The Fire Star will grow up first and then come to meet you again in another form. By then, you will know you are the She-Fire Star.

You will challenge the He-Fire Star for control of the clan. But it may not be seen by all as a challenge, not on this level. Fire Star, he will feel it, he does already. But your challenge will be on many levels of time and space, barely here, but here. The challenge will be a necessary rebalancing, for our times."

None of this made sense at that time. "Please, I don't want to see him. I don't want to talk to him. Help me get out of here." I could feel terror pouring from my eyes into Kiowa's heart. And then I felt so dizzy that I began to stumble and fall.

Kiowa caught me in mid-air. He froze, holding me in that position – and looked me in the eye until I looked back. This is how he got my attention. Finally he asked me to sit down. He held my arms so that I could do so without losing my balance. He still held my gaze. He again had tears in his eyes. "I feel great shame. I am ashamed of my medicine brother. Can you hear me now?"

I nodded yes.

Kiowa held my gaze with that blazing blue light coming out of his eyes. "Ask me, right now, ask me: 'Is it safe, Kiowa?' Come on, ask me."

I echoed his question. "Kiowa, is it safe?"

"Yes. Your spirit is safe. And your spirit guards your flesh. Your flesh is safe. He cannot have you now."

"I couldn't do it again, especially not now, not now. Never."

"You won't let it happen again. Close your eyes and look at the two of us sitting here. There are guards around us. Look at them.

Mountain lions and wolves form a circle of protection for you tonight."

I quieted my shakes. "I see something amazing behind the ring of animals."

"What do you see?"

I squinted as if to see them better. "Well, I know these beings. They are the Seven spirits. They saved my life." I exclaimed, "Ancient priestesses or something!"

"I see them, too."

"That's my family, Kiowa. I am of them. They're me. They're from my home out there."

Kiowa's eyes widened. "I know. I see. I can tell." Kiowa took my hand. "This vision is the sign we have awaited." He made a slight bow of acknowledgement to me.

I was a bit taken aback by this pronouncement and show of strange formality in his bow, but more taken by the vision itself and the return of the Seven presences to my sight.

And then there was more to see. "I see something else there. It's in the middle of the circle," I told him.

"What do you see?"

"An owl … and a dove," I said astonished.

"Who are they?" he asked.

"They are you and me. You, an owl and me, a dove."

"And we can fly away if we need to," he told me serenely. The sound of his voice moved me through the space around us, as if that voice itself was a boat on a river of air.

I sat down on the dirt and hugged my knees to my chest. I rocked myself, a finally conscious fetus. Kiowa stood guard, protecting my spirit from intrusion until I could understand that I could do the same for myself.

"Later we will go to the sweat lodge."

I saw Gun in the distance.

"Kiowa, it's good that you're here. You're different. You're like me. Gun knows this."

"Gun is my power brother. He helped me get free from a cement box."

"A what?"

"I will tell you sometime."

Kiowa and I saw Gun looking at me. Even from the distance, I could feel in my heart what Gun was seeing, and also what he was thinking: There I was, the young and unwilling medicine woman to-be who didn't know who she was and didn't have much of a self, trying to organize the spirits coming through her. There I was, half dressed, breasts painted and hair adorned, wearing a loincloth, the look of the spirits in my eyes. I heard Gun think he could love this woman. But he would not take her for she was not his, nor was she even Mark's, nor was she Kiowa's. She was her own, and she should learn this as early as possible in her life, at least before the big changes coming on Earth.

Whoever "she" was, I thought to myself. Am I the "she?"

Kiowa smiled as if he heard me wonder. He nodded at Gun.

"So, here is my young white goddess."

Fire Star startled us both, even Kiowa. Fire Star had popped out of the liquid of people so suddenly, as if he had moved from the far side of the bowl to this spot without walking. I felt an acute worry at that moment. I worried that this Fire Star, renowned as the keeper of the planetary survival knowledge, was a torrid sorcerer like the kind I remembered from my childhood fairy tales, one who would have all power over me.

But, just then, on the tail of that worried thought, I heard Kiowa thinking, telling me without words, to remember that my spirit was as strong as Fire Star's. Stronger. No one could have me. I was my own. And I was of those priestesses. They and I were one. It was time for me to be the She-Fire Star and accept the transfer of power bestowed upon me.

I couldn't make much sense of this awesome bit of information; however, I swallowed the ball of saliva that had collected in my mouth, and resolutely turned my concentration deep into Fire Star's eyes. I was a dove, I could fly away, but I stayed still. I put the mountain lions and the wolves in front of my spirit. They bared their teeth at the Fire Star. And I saw the Seven looming above me, their quiet presence a definite force I could learn to call upon. I was quite surprised to find myself doing this, and to be understanding what I was doing.

Fire Star himself looked quite surprised. He seemed to feel me protect myself. He grinned awkwardly for just a moment, and then his face went stone cold. He turned up his dark power. He glowered deep into me until I felt a chill stab itself right in my heart. I heard Kiowa

105

say something to me like "don't quit," but I knew Kiowa wasn't really speaking out loud, his words were sounding inside my head. I sent the chill of Fire Star outside of my body and away like a river flowing onto other parts of the Earth. I stood my ground.

"Your mother did not teach you well," the Fire Star growled at me. There was now a whole circle of people standing around us, listening. I sensed they were confused by this standoff between their leader and a teenage girl. Fire Star went on with force: "We must change your name … tonight."

Fire Star glanced at Kiowa with a look of deep disapproval. "These are not things to teach these white squaws." The flame of insult rose within me. He had dishonored me by calling me "squaw" which I had heard actually meant prostitute or something derogatory about women or about the feminine. No one should be called squaw now. Although the roots of the word are debated, this word has come to be demeaning.

Now Kiowa looked at Fire Star with disapproval, reacting to his words. "This woman knows medicine ways of her own accord. She is here for good reason and you know it. I see that the power already lies within her. But we can make no claim to even our own magic. It is of the Earth and stars for the use of all … all, I hope, of good heart."

"In this, you fail your people, Kiowa. This white girl cannot know what she knows if you do not show her that she knows it. This teaching will end now."

Kiowa stood his ground solidly against Fire Star, shaking his head no.

Fire Star looked faintly surprised at Kiowa's resistance, but covered it up with assertive talk. "You have no place by this woman. My word is say here. I have taken her for mine. She carries my seed now."

As I reeled with humiliation, Kiowa and Fire Star locked gazes, in the middle of the circle of people witnessing their encounter. Neither man moved as time passed – more time, timeless time. At least ten minutes went by.

During that time, the some thirty people gathered around them began to chant. I watched from the side. I could feel the energy locked between these two men. I could see it, two men in combat embrace, a frozen dance of steel icicles – a silent rebalancing of their powers. I wanted to learn to do this. I knew I needed to learn this. But maybe women do this differently, I told myself.

As quickly as it had begun, the match was over. The two men broke their gazes with a start and turned away from each other simultaneously. The two of them walked off in different directions. Was this a standoff or a resolution? I, the dove, wondered. I figured that I would have flown away, retreated, and lost to that Fire Star man – that I would never have lasted so long as Kiowa. I knew right then that if it were somehow true that I was really supposed to be a part of all this, I would need to find my power before I could do whatever my Work was, here on this planet.

Kiowa returned suddenly to my side, and announced to me, "The sweat lodge is fired up. You'll want to be there."

I clenched my teeth. I wasn't sure why, but this sounded like a bad idea. "No. I won't want to be there."

"You'll be alright. The rebalancing has already begun. You have come for this purpose … to help begin the rebalancing, to bring on, and help guide, the Great Return."

Great Return? No! My head ached. I wanted to deny all this stuff now and just get away from it. "No, really, I'm not who you think I am, whoever that is. I haven't come for any such thing."

Kiowa chuckled softly. "I know this is difficult, very difficult. Great learnings can be that way, very much that way. But, you will see, in time, you will see. You will see who you are."

"Why me? Why do you say it is me? How could you possibly be so certain?"

"Because it is *you* who are so certain. You came to us, not we to you. You have finally returned. It is written in the air around you. I see it in the spirits who walk with you. It is in the color of your light."

"Really, come on, please, let's stop this now."

"This is not up to me. I am just a guide come to help along your way. You actually called me to you."

"No, I did not, Kiowa, really. I never met you before I got here. Never."

"I am only here to remind you that you have made this choice – this commitment – long, long ago. And you will come to know this better than anyone around you."

I struggled with this. Testing a truth can be like this. Moments of uncertainty are a must along the way. "Kiowa, if this is true, then tell me when I will come to know. When? Exactly when?" Was all this right? Was all this logical? Was all this true? I tried to call on my mental faculties as they had worked outside the Tribe. This was not easy for me to do.

"You will tell us all when as you yourself come to know when. You will share your visions with the people, with people everywhere."

I looked doubtful.

Kiowa put his hands on my shoulders. "Now, go into the sweat and see for us all."

I frowned, confused, upset, shaken by all that had happened. My reality was no longer what it had been. It would never be the same. And I would never be the same. But who would I be?

Kiowa urged me on to the next level. "Now the next step is the sweat. Too often, this sacred ritual is abused by those who do not really understand it. For example, too many white men and even white women pose as medicine people or shamans and say they lead sacred sweats when they do not. Some of our own people do this too. And, even when done right, sometimes people need to do it several, many many, times before they understand the great spiritual meaning of the sweat. The sweat lodge is a sacred place for prayer. The Lakota Sioux call it the *inipi*. You sit with the Earth, real close in to her, in her womb. Ancestors come in visions, tonight with truth about the future Earth changes and with visions of your purpose here. Sometimes the truth comes and tests you. Sometimes it plants itself like a seed unfolding many years later."

I shook my head no. I wasn't going in. No way.

Kiowa smiled. "Okay then, I will make it easy for you to go for this sacred opportunity. Go in if you want to see Mark."

Mark? I felt a wave of relief. "Mark! Okay then. Finally."

I started walking. Kiowa was right behind me. I felt him thinking about me, good loving thoughts. I turned to him, smiled and wanted to hug him. "I want to hug you and to thank you for everything."

"Good," he said, and I did. I felt us merge again – waves of rainbows emanated from our bodies. The edges between us dissolved. In that moment, I looked at Kiowa, as if to say I loved him, as if to reach him with my heart. I was surprised at myself. But he was not.

However, he shook his head no. "I am only your guide, your scout. I only come to share truth and to see you safe passage. This is my role this lifetime here. I am an owl, you are a dove. We are not the same species. We cannot mate." Kiowa looked slightly pained at this.

"I didn't mean mate," I whispered. I was embarrassed.

Kiowa smiled. "Yes, you did mean mate, young white medicine woman from the stars, white wing. That is what that energy is about. I am honored. All chiefs love such riches as yours. Be careful how you share these. Be careful where you show them. Keep your fertile spirit soil protected."

Somehow, when he told me this, it did not sound demeaning or teasing or in any way disrespectful. We smiled softly at each other, I, still slightly embarrassed, he, obviously honored at my subtle expression of interest, maybe even of desire.

Then he tipped his head to the side. "Now you have another adventure … the sweat, the place of purification, where all enter as embryos. This is a very old tradition, a very special one. Although I wonder sometimes if all these changes Fire Star is making in this ceremony preserve its sacred power…."

Kiowa led me to the outside door of a large canvas, plastic tarp, and animal skin covered dome-shaped tent. Before entering, women came over to me and waved some kind of burning bundle smelling like smoking sage around me. One of the women was telling me that this was *pe-ji-ho-ta*. Then I was given a ceremonial pipe of medicine weed to smoke, and more of that tea to drink. Some strange words were said by dancing women who moved around me in a circle. They were saying something thanking someone, maybe their Creator. I caught and actually recognized a few phrases: "*Wakan Tanka … Mitakuye Oyasin … Ah-ho. Aho.*"

Aho.

9.
waiving womb

The door flapped open…

… as if to beckon me to cross another threshold. Kiowa gently pushed me in. "I may come in later," he said when I reached back for him. "Find your Mark," he said strongly yet wistfully.

I went through that doorway into the dark womb of the sweat lodge. I couldn't help feeling that it was a little like descending into hell. But was the hell just fear? I crouched near the entrance while a few new hot stones were passed in from someone outside – apparently the firekeeper – to the pile of stones in the center. In the smoke and steam, I saw a circle of bodies. Lost and already too hot, I crawled over the dirt floor and sat near the wall, joining the circle. Then the flap to the dome was closed. Now it was unimaginably dark and beastly hot. Kiowa seemed an eternity away. I focused on my breathing to stay centered. This was very helpful, and a good learning itself.

Water was poured onto the hot rocks. The resulting wave of steam was so thick that there seemed to be no air to breath. I was about to panic when, "Hey, Lilith, Lil'," a voice whispered in the dark. It was Mark, a few people away. "It's me."

Mark! Relief and great joy raced through me. I started to sob and to move over toward Mark's voice, to sit next to Mark. But, at that moment, a large body moved in front of me and put its hand on me, pressing me down into the ground. Even in the pitch black dark I knew it was Fire Star. Chief Fire Star. I froze. My guts wrenched.

Mark did nothing. Perhaps he didn't know what Fire Star had done to me. Mark's shadow was simple and clear, but it was small and off to the side and not prepared to defend me.

I felt desperately lost. There I was in the wilderness of my soul. Or of someone's soul, most likely humanity's. The people on either side of me cleared away. Fire Star sat by me. It was pretty dark and when the door to the sweat lodge was closed it was darker. Fire Star put his paw firmly on my crotch. I could feel he would not remove it until he wanted to.

I was silent. I felt like a dying white dove in a dark airless cage. Trapped. And I was so hot that I thought I would die. I could barely breathe. I couldn't feel the sacred beauty of the *inipi*. Sweat beaded out of every pore. The paint on my face and breasts began to run. Cups of tea came around. I was very thirsty, but I turned the liquid down. I wanted to clear my mind. No more peyote tea. His hand was still on me.

Finally responding to the powerful pull of the Earth, I lay on the ground now, dizzy and panting. This dark womb was consuming me. I wanted to die and heard my mind saying, "Mother Earth, take me back, send me home" over and over. I could hardly see, so I closed my eyes. Fire Star's hands and his troubling shadow were all over me, claiming his territory. Mark did nothing. No one else stopped this. Kiowa was not in there. Where could he be? Why wasn't Kiowa here to stop Fire Star's abuse of the sacred?

Fire Star's hand was still on me. The tea came around again. I was so thirsty that I sat up and accepted it. Now it tasted different. It was much stronger. The tent was filled with the smell of medicine weed. I couldn't find air to breathe that did not contain medicine weed smoke. I felt too dizzy to stand up and leave, or to crawl out and leave – I could hardly move. And all I could see were colored shadows – colored shadows and Fire Star's strange silhouette.

The flap opened and some women crawled in, chanting. Behind them came some men, chanting in deeper voices. I felt a bit of cool oxygen-laden air trickle into my lungs. But then, the flap closed and the ember light emanating from the hot stones in the center was the only light available. Now people inside were singing in very high, higher than I had ever heard, tones. Their serene yet ecstatic voices sounded to me like a choir of the most exalted angels. I wanted this exquisitely exhilarating magnetic beauty to fully envelope me, to transport me into heaven or some place like it, but I was afraid of Fire Star and could not let go enough to access the ecstasy. Still, I could feel that the voices were bringing a light-filled doorway or window into focus. They were bringing a doorway to pure sheer light into the lower darkness. I desperately wanted to go through the opening to the spirit realm, but I could not let go.

Everything became silhouette and shadow. And we were all unbelievably crowded together now. I kept thinking I would go insane. Fire Star's claw was still on me. Hand ... claw ... it was changing form I thought. I then realized that, if I did go through the portal to the light, into the spirit realm, Fire Star would go through that portal with me. He would follow me into that majestic dimension, track me, hold onto me, weigh me down. I could not let that happen.

There was silence for a while. People must die in these sweat lodges, I told myself furtively, that's what they mean by purification – death. And then, suddenly, I found myself craving purification, whatever it was. I would die to then survive. But I was not dying, just moving into a new phase of my life. This was the sort of thing rattling around in my brain.

"The naming," Fire Star suddenly announced, lifting his hand from me for the moment. He moved closer to the hot stones, which were steaming in the center of the tent, and began to sing a song in a language I didn't understand. My reflex to his initiation of this naming ceremony was to try to get out of there as quickly as possible. I tried to move to crawl out, but felt too sick to my stomach to manage this. And Fire Star's powerful chanting seemed to be filling my brain until I had no self left.

I frantically searched for my self, with my mind racing through my head and body. "Your self is hiding in your heart," a voice said inside my head. It was a very loud, very kind, bell-like, resonant voice, made up of Seven voices speaking to me in unison. "Look there, in your heart, where the doorway to your home is," the voice said.

This was hard to do, not having a self available to send to look for my self. However, I somehow grabbed onto a tiny idea, a picture of a very small person running along the veins toward my heart, using these as a map. I ran and ran – finally, I was in it, I was in my heart, I was inside what I could find of my *self*. It wasn't much but it was enough of a self to feel I had one.

And suddenly I realized – my self was hiding, nestled within the crystallized drop of water that spirit, Sveeka, my mother, had given me several nights ago, when I lay in desperation in Fire Star's bed throne. Sveeka! Sveeka! Is this crystal a doorway? A star ship? In my mind I saw a doorway open. And beyond it, I saw the Seven stars – the Seven sister stars.

Just as I found myself at this awesome doorway, I felt my physical body being lifted and pulled toward Fire Star by several people's hands. My attention was back in the hot sweat lodge. Fire Star was chanting something I couldn't make sense of. A man next to him said, "What will be this woman's name?" in a monotone.

Fire Star turned to me, his fire lit eyes scrutinizing me as if someone were scraping me inside and out with sandpaper. Then he closed his eyes and seemed to be whispering to someone who wasn't there. His Fire Star shaped shadow seemed to be meeting shadows that had no bodies. Were they those warriors that had wanted me dead in all dimensions?

Thoughts were flitting through my mind and evaporating as rapidly as the embers flying up from the hot stones in the center were disappearing. But one thought was immediately very pronounced and lasting: I did not want a new name from Fire Star. This must *not* happen. Somehow, I knew that if I let him name me, I would not be able to do my Work, whatever that was. My role in the Great Return, whatever that was, would be compromised – blocked.

As soon as this rebellious thought coalesced within my psyche, I felt something hit me. Something happened to my mind. An invisible hot claw reached in and grabbed my self and squeezed it real hard. I felt myself melting away to nothing – something very big and very powerful, a force that I could not understand and that I did not like, seemed to be drinking my self away from me.

In desperation, I called for those Seven voices, the voices speaking in unison that I had heard within my self a few minutes prior. I screamed inside my mind. Come voices. Come voice! Come! Seven Come! Priestesses where are you?

My head pounded in immense pain. I heard my self tell my self that I had to believe in the Seven-in-one voice harder in order to bring it to me. Believing was being. Believing was the key. So then, I felt myself believe even harder that there really was such a voice.

Sure enough, as soon as I did fully believe, the voice of the Seven arrived back with such full force that it almost knocked me out. The voice came like a blast of air within me. The Seven spoke to me from deep, deep within me, from a place deeper than I had ever imagined existed. In my head, I heard the Seven speak to me in the first person, as if I were speaking to myself: "I ... I am ... Akashakana ... the priestess of ... . I am ... I am ... the fire dove ... I can fly away on wings of white light. But I am strong and I can stay without being captive. I am a dove. I am a dove. I am the dove. I am the dove. I am the dove. I am the dove. I am the dove. I am the dove. I am the dove. I am the *fire dove*, Akashakana. I am. I am I am. I am I am I am I am."

The voice within me halted a moment and I became aware that Fire Star's voice was completing a chant, and now saying, "This woman's name will be —"

Then, with such a ferocity that human words cannot describe it, that blasting air pounded right into me, its whipping cold wind driving in through the top of my skull and rushing out my mouth, interrupting Fire Star and loudly completing his sentence: "I ... I am ... I am ... *to name ... myself!*"

Abruptly, I realized what I was doing, how this must have sounded. I was so embarrassed, I thought I would die. But I knew that my Seven priestesses had spoken. Who was I to deny their massive power?

Now I whispered hoarsely, "My Seven ... guides ... have ... spoken. I ... I am ... Akashakana."

Fire Star was silent. Everyone was silent. Things seemed to collapse. What I was doing was so wrong and so disrespectful that it was unheard of, I could tell. Somehow, even the people outside the tent felt what had happened. Their drumming stopped.

The Seven had spoken. The ancient Akashakana had risen again, this time here, through me.

Filled with a short burst of strength, I pushed the Fire Star and the others off of me and crawled out of the tent. It seemed that everyone was seeing me, their eyes looking into me.

I felt more naked than even my bare skin revealed. I wanted to fly away but couldn't find my wings yet, like a baby dove just born into the world.

Once outside the sweat lodge, fresh air filled my lungs. I saw Gun a few feet away. I saw Kiowa moving toward me and I fainted into his arms. Just as I lost consciousness, I felt the cool rush of angel wings across my heart.

Somewhere on the far side of the night sky, a star burst.

Akashakana.

10.
crying tree

I awoke with my own name.

It was the morning after I had passed out. Now I found myself in the same place, but in what I was now sure was enemy territory. I found myself being blinded by a harsh ray of sunlight breaking through a crack in a rotting wooden wall. I realized that someone had dressed me. Probably Kiowa. Where did he go?

I heard myself whimpering and felt myself pushing my hands against some man who was leaning over me. He grabbed my hands and held them down.

"What are you doing?" the man said. "It's me, Mark." I still struggled against him. He shook me. "Hey, come on. It's just me. You need to wake up and drink some water."

I suddenly realized that this was indeed Mark's voice. Nevertheless, I barked, "Let go of me!" He did. I pushed him away. My eyes were still adjusting to the light and I couldn't see his face, but I knew he felt he'd been unfairly scolded.

I squinted at him. "Don't get close to me when I'm asleep," I begged and closed my eyes again. "Don't."

He moved farther away and settled onto his knees. "But you always used to like it."

"I don't any more. So don't."

"Sorry."

I opened my eyes again and could see this time. I was in the barn where I had left my things. I was very cold, cold to the bone. I'd been sleeping on the cracked wooden floor. I didn't feel right. I shuddered visibly.

"God, what's wrong with you?" Mark asked, sounding a combination of angry and worried.

"I said don't, Mark. That's all. Don't." I looked at him. Young – also eighteen – handsome, brown skinned, thick long brown hair. A beautiful young man. I felt a real deep sibling-like affection for him, but I shoved him away.

"What's wrong with you? You always liked me near you before."

"That was before. Everything's different now."

"How? You're the same. I'm the same."

I couldn't believe he really didn't get it. "I did it. I did it for you."

"What're you saying? Did what? You're not making sense," Mark scolded. "Have some water, go back to sleep. I'll try again later. Or maybe you just don't want me anymore."

"Mark … he made it like I had to do it. Had to … in order to stay … to be part of this … to come here to you." My eyes welled up with tears. I was cold and groggy and upset – and I wanted Mark to do something about what had happened.

"Who? What *are you* talking about?"

"Fire Star, your hero," I announced sarcastically, although Fire Star had been my hero, too.

Mark looked as if I'd hit him. "You have to explain better. You're accusing him of something … I'm not sure what, but it sounds like something he just wouldn't do." Mark paused and then continued, "Unless the spirits told him he had to."

"Oh, come on Mark. That's such bullshit." I studied him. "What's happened to you? The look in your eyes is different." I scrutinized his face harder. "You must have been brainwashed or something. Don't you get it? He made me have sex with him! I didn't like it. I didn't want it. I feel sick about it. Horrible! Disgusted!"

Now I could see insult written all over Mark's eyelids as he scanned the ground next to me. He removed the possibility of eye contact from our communication, as if he didn't want me to reach him.

Finally he sighed and without looking up, said, "I don't know how to feel about that. But he's a great, great man. He sees the future. And this place is my life now. He runs this Tribe. I have joined it. I am a member. For life."

"How can you just shrug this off? How can you let him get away with it? He's done it to lots of girls. Don't any of the guys care?"

"I bet you could've said no to him," Mark accused. And then his voice trailed off into thought, his eyes still glued to the floor, as if he was avoiding looking at me at all costs.

"I couldn't. He had a gun."

"If you really wanted to, you could've said no," he accused again, still refusing to see me.

"Don't you care that he did this to me?" I accused him. "To your girlfriend? Why don't you get angry at him – not me?"

"Shhh. You'll get us kicked out of here."

"Mark, he violated me. He could have shot me." Silence. "I'm telling you, your Fire Star strangled me. I almost died. I did die!" I still couldn't get through to Mark. "Mark. Where are you? Where's your head? What's happened to your heart? You've never treated me like this before."

"Well, you're not dead are you? And, about the rest of it, you let him do it." Mark was fully angry now and blaming me for what had happened.

"No, you're very wrong, Mark." I gritted my teeth.

Then silence.

Minutes passed by, seeming like hours. I stared at the top of Mark's head, wondering what had happened to his mind here. Mark finally yanked his eyes from their iron link to the ground. Now I could see the deep pain in his eyes. He was trying not to cry. He was a man, yes, but still a young man, and this was far too difficult for him to know how to handle. He rubbed his eyes, as if they had dust in them. He didn't want me to think he was going to cry.

And then he spoke more gently, "Please, I'm sorry. Really. God, oh God …." He paused, seeming to struggle with himself. He cleared his throat and looked strong again. "But I mean, well, okay, it happened. It wasn't good. It wasn't your fault. I believe you." He touched my hand.

I was silent although I knew he wanted me to forgive him for blaming me.

He went on, "And, tell you the truth, I'm not happy about it. I'm shocked … and you're not very happy about it. You're very mad. And we're confused about it together. I mean, we never ever even talked about either of us being with anyone else. We haven't exactly even really been together, not all the way. Not really. I guess I never thought either of us would be with anyone else."

He waited for me to say something but I didn't. I just curled up like a fetus.

Mark got down off his knees, sat and crossed his legs, and went on. "But these people, well they, well, I guess everyone around here does that. Does it with more than one person. But we don't have to. It isn't an iron rule or something."

I cleared my throat and tried not to cry. "Mark, I'm leaving. I came here for you. You. But now you're different. You aren't you anymore."

"I don't know how you think you'll get out. It's a long, long, maybe thirty miles or more long, really rough dirt road out. And rides out hardly ever come. They just don't want—"

I interrupted. "I'll make someone take me out," I said again.

"The car they keep here doesn't work."

"I'll make someone take me out."

"No one will. It's like crossing a forbidden boundary."

"I'm going. That's that." I was determined.

"Please, let's us two make this thing, this being here, work if we can. It's everything we believe in. If it turns out not to work, we'll quit. I won't let it happen again. I don't want anyone else to have you ever again. Not even him."

"Mark, he's not some big hero. He's just a creepy guy. He doesn't want justice – not for women anyway." It was obvious that Mark didn't want to hear me say this. I wanted to shake him and wake him up, but I knew that would make no difference. In his eyes, in his voice – I could tell that, somehow, he was just gone. "Mark, I don't know if I can make it with you, make love with you, with anyone now. Ever."

He looked surprised. This wasn't part of the bargain. But he said, "You will. It'll be okay. You'll see. It'll just take a while. Things will get better. You'll feel okay again. I promise. I'll take care of you."

"Well, I don't want you to push me about it. It might be a while. I mean days or weeks or longer, Mark."

"It's okay, I'll wait. We had something good started, we were real close. Everyone thought we were twin brother and sister, we look and sound so much alike. Remember?"

I nodded yes.

"We'll be good together again. It'll come back."

I hoped so, but I had no hope to offer Mark right then. A hollow nauseated feeling filled my gut. I thought I might throw up, so I got up and stepped out of the barn – into the Tribe's world, the land where time was doing strange things – the land where people tried to go back to the past, or what they could reenact of that lifestyle, in order to survive the future. And I was stuck in this utopia waiting to happen, this fortress: Fire Star Tribe Land, location #3, Pantribal America. But it was the self-proclaimed leader, Chief Fire Star, holding me captive, not everyone else there.

A breeze whisked by and the fresh smell of pine trees filled my nostrils. I was instantly refreshed, cleansed, and taken aback by the wonderful sensation. I relaxed just a second, and in washed the remarkable beauty of those woods and their mountains and the sky blanketing them. The loud majesty of this land lifted her veil and hit me. I could see how it could cast a spell on the people who walked it. Wow, what a place, I told myself. Even though I didn't want myself to love it, I could hear the land calling me to walk upon her, to touch the Earth and her wonders. Obeying the insistent call, I took a few steps to the west, heading across the lush green meadow.

And then I stopped short. My feet were buzzing. The ground was charged again – the way it had been when I first got there with Gun! But this time it was a gentler charge and I could walk comfortably, even take in energy from the Earth beneath my feet. I took a few more steps, testing the intensity of this strange energy. It remained gentle enough to step on. I even liked the feel.

But, a few steps later, my ears were suddenly filled with the shrill sound of a child crying. My feet took me closer and closer to that sound until its source was in sight. At that point, I froze. What in the hell was I seeing? A toddler left to scream alone on a high tree stump? A few adults were in the distance, busy with other activities, but obviously aware of the child's plight. I watched, horrified.

The cries shifted to wails and then to screams. I stood there watching as the screams became excruciating shrieks. I felt painfully although confusingly connected with the child's plight. Finally I couldn't stand it anymore. I ran over to the stump, reached for the child, and said, "Come on, baby, let me get you down."

Just as the child's anguished cries ceased and he stepped a tentative step toward me, a firm hand came from behind me, planted itself on my shoulder, and yanked me away from the child. The child sat down there, up on the stump, and stopped crying.

"What are you doing?" the voice attached to the hand said.

I whirled around and found a very tall, large, fat, angry white man towering over me. I looked up into his unpleasant face and said, "Well, if it's really any of your business, I'm helping this poor child of course. Something you could have done before I got here if you could've been bothered."

I turned around to get the child again. This time, the fat man's hand yanked me away so hard that I fell to the ground. "Who do you think you are?" he shouted.

He helped me up and looked at me closely. Then he gulped and said, slightly embarrassed, "Oh, gee, you must be the girl Gun brought up – the predicted girl."

The child started to shriek again. I again made a move to rescue the boy. The fat man again stopped me, although more gently this time. "Hey you, that's MY son."

Now a smaller finer hand came from behind him. "Stan, leave her be. She doesn't know what it's about." He took his hand off me right away.

A beautiful Native American woman stepped out from behind him. I saw her precisely chiseled high cheekbones and noble poise and thought to myself that she must be a queen of something. She extended her hand to greet me. "I am Singing Brook Woman, from the Tslagee or what you probably call Cherokee Tribe, and this crying child is my son too."

"But, why has he been left here to cry?" I asked her. I didn't add that I had some Tsalagee in me too.

Singing Brook patted the cut tree affectionately, as if it were a pet. "This is the crying stump. It is old way tradition to put a crying child on the crying stump until the child stops crying. The young one learns what we all must remember: that it is not our tears that bring us needed changes."

The three of us realized the child hadn't been crying for a while. Each of the three of us raised our eyebrows and looked over at the boy at the same time. Singing Brook took her son down and put him on the ground. He toddled off some distance out of arm's reach, and then turned to watch us.

"But it seems so—" I started to tell her.

"It did to me too, at first …" Stan, the big white man, broke in, "… but these days I appreciate the Tribe's ways. These revival children are raised strong and stoic, not flaccid and wimpy like white kids."

He saw me staring at his fat gut. "Not like me," he apologized for himself.

For some reason, I felt I was still linked to this child's plight. "Well, not to be critical or anything, but there has to be some other way to train kids, some other way to learn important lessons, a way other than pain and humiliation."

Singing Brook smiled with deep understanding. "Well, this is one of our ways to teach and train. It builds strength, fortitude and insight. It prepares children for the biggest journeys they will take."

For a moment, I heard Kiowa's voice telling me about the Seven sisters riding that tree stump into the sky. A brief flicker of recognition must have raced through my face, because Singing Brook seemed to catch it and seemed to acknowledge it. She put her hand on my shoulder. "I think you get what I mean."

"Not really," I said. I really didn't.

"Oh, it's okay," she smiled. "Look, it is already good enough that you care for the children. Many people do not even see the children. But you do. This is already a gift to us."

I shrugged off the compliment because it didn't really mean anything to me. Or did it?

"But you see," she continued, "we are a different people than yours, or than those you think you belong to. Our ways are different and our needs are different. Like yours, we are a dying people, but for different reasons. If we don't return to our old ways of raising strong, tough, stoic braves and brave women, we will die – our people will die. Our knowledge, brought here from the stars, will die – and the planet will die with us. We have already allowed ourselves to weaken after so many years in captivity."

"Captivity? What are you talking about?"

"The Rez – reservation life," she said. "And the prison of your culture. You free people have never known captivity."

I nodded – but it would be a while before the full experience of being a captive – in my case, the Tribe's captive – would hit me hard. Then I would know firsthand what it might mean to have one's freedom removed, even with all the so-called right reasons given.

Singing Brook and her man, Stan, invited me to share their meal with them. I hadn't eaten in so long, I couldn't remember when, so I said yes. While we were eating, Singing Brook looked at Stan and waved her head in the direction of the field. Stan caught the message, stood up and took his son out into the field with their food. I gathered she wanted to talk to me alone.

"There are some things I would like to share with you," she said in a very gentle voice. "What's happening just now is very important. As with Stan and myself, we here are mixing our blood among our tribes, crossing the tribes to build one bigger better Tribe. And we are mixing our red blood with white blood, to save both our races. And other bloods to save other races. The red tribes -- we carry in our genes certain survival wisdom that is going to be needed by all humans, wisdom written on the code we brought here within us, from the ancient star worlds."

"Yes," I said, perhaps not overly attentive just then. "I read about this in articles about Fire Star's and other people's teachings." I watched Stan and their son, across the meadow, throwing tomahawks at rocks. Singing Brook was wanting me to pay more attention to what she was trying to tell me – she put her hand on my knee and I looked back at her. "Perhaps you have read words. But, you can listen now with your heart. The new Tribe will be of many colors … a true rainbow race. This will be the surviving Tribe, and I want to tell you, we see you as the white woman who has come to carry on the noble blood, to carry it into many worlds."

I felt myself recoil at her words – and spoke without thinking. "Me? Well, I don't think so. Not really. I'm just here for a while, with Mark, my boyfriend. And we aren't having a baby."

She reached out, pointed to my abdomen area, and looked me in the eye. I forced myself to look away.

Just then we both saw five somber men – the same burly men who had appeared out of nowhere to greet Gun and me when I first arrived. Now they were walking toward us from across the meadow, appearing out of nowhere, still carrying their rifles. A slow chill made its way through me.

Singing Brook saw my reaction. She herself didn't look very happy about their presence. She forced a tiny laugh and then asked me if I minded if she said a prayer.

"No, of course not … if you think that'll make a difference."

"When Creator is called for protection … just for the calling, Creator comes."

She prayed for a while in her own language. I pretended not to see the men walking through the meadow. I closed my eyes. After a while, I actually found myself swaying in the rhythm of her chant. Then she was done.

I opened my eyes. The team of five armed men were standing over us. The biggest one spoke to me. "Fire Star wants to see you. Come with us."

He grabbed my arm and pulled me onto my feet. I yanked away from him. He reached to grab me again. Brook's hand caught his and stopped it in mid-air.

"No. I will take her down," Brook, now standing, instructed him calmly.

"She will come with us," the main armed man answered. He turned back to me and glowered. I looked away, not wanting more eye contact with him. Brook stood between the men and me. "No. I take her. That is the word. We are done speaking with you. You can leave us now."

The biggest man looked down at Singing Brook. She stared unusually coolly back up at him, and he seemed suddenly unsure of himself. He froze for a moment. Then he shrugged and turned, beckoning the men to follow, and stomped away.

"Oh, thanks a lot. I don't like those guys, and I don't want to go." I took a deep breath.

"Well," Singing Brook said, "you don't really want to mess with them. They think they are in charge here. Like rez police or something, they're supposed to keep intruders out, people who would bother us. But they get carried away. They shouldn't have guns. Thing is, they're hiding some of the Underground here ... and the Underground thanks us with guns."

"The underground? What's that?"

"The Silver Underground. You probably heard about them in the news. That's where all the guns came from. There's a huge stash here. I'll sneak and show you sometime. They say they're teaching revolutionary tactics, building a strong underground militia, ready for revolution if need be. I don't agree that this is good. I say violence is not the way ... that the physical violence standard is a man's way, and that the man's way will kill all of us off. But I stay out of their way. It is better to stay calm with them and tell them what you want straight out, calmly but strongly, no anger, no threat. But no feeling afraid either."

"Well that might work for you, but I doubt it would for me." I looked around to be sure they were gone.

"Maybe not quite yet. But you will learn. You must, because it will be the women who will pull this planet through the big transition and into the next era … the women of all tribes. Women like you and me are the Great Return, right?"

She paused. I said nothing. The Great Return again. What could this thing be?

"You know what I am talking about."

"No," I said and I thought I meant it. What exactly was she talking about?

"I think you do know. You just forget you know, that's all. You are the one they said was coming."

"Really? You think this? I'm just an everyday person. And a white girl. Well, white and not white."

Singing Brook laughed. "An everyday person? Well, of course you are. You have to be to make it through and do your Work. But take a look at your own bone structure – not your skin and eyes, your bone structure – and you tell me that you don't know you are one of us."

"I don't know about all this," I ventured, trying to decide what to say. Was I, wasn't I, one of them?

"Well, learn it well and right away, girl. We need you to wake up. It will soon be our time, so you must learn to confront and back down the old male power. Learn what you have to learn not to be killed. Please do not get killed."

"Killed! I hope not."

"Takes more than hoping. Look around. Yes, this is a beautiful place and some beautiful things are happening here. But you have to hold your true spirit … what you are really about … close in tight and protect it. You have to shield yourself, for all our sakes, especially when you confront the male Star ... and watch your back. Listen ... live right now in each now ... with Creator at your side. Each new step you take, pray for guidance. This will keep you safe."

"Safe..." I mulled this all over.

"And call the Seven Sisters when ever you need them."

"The Seven? I—" So she knew of the Seven!

"But wait. Now you must go see the Fire Star. Challenge him for control of the clan. Take back the medicine power. Women are counting on you. We are all being called to help bring on this great rebalancing, the great return of truth."

All this sounded important, but I was now quite panicked at the idea of confronting Fire Star again. Still, what was this power thing that Singing Brook was talking about? "But ... how will I know what to do?" I asked.

"Just look and listen, always look and listen to the signs and sounds around you. Quiet little signs are everywhere, always coming. But most of them are missed. And watch everything you do and think. Each little move you make must be a piece of prayer." She consciously turned her head toward the sun, and closed her eyes. "After a while, answers, guiding messages, will come to you."

As I watched, she carefully extended her right hand palm down toward the ground between her feet, and then her left hand palm up directly over her head to the sky. Then she slowly moved both her hands so that their palms were on either side of her head, facing the sun, and made a sound: "Mmmmmmm." Then her hands moved so that the right could cradle the left, palms up, in the space right below her left breast.

I watched her beautiful prayer dance – somehow her motions made what she'd been telling me in words come alive. Her eyes opened again, and she looked so deeply into mine that I thought she would look right through me: "Each move," she told me, "will be directed by spirit." Now both her hands covered her heart. "Signs will be clear then."

Quickly now both her hands moved right to me where they pressed on my abdomen. "Spirit will cause you to see these signs." She dropped her hands. "Watch for signs, follow them … stay on the path. Never forget why you are here. We need you to do this. You are an important key in the Great Return. We all are. Walk with we women who are here living these lifetimes now for this same reason as you are."

I sighed. I really could not wrap my mind around all this.

"Don't worry, you will always be shown the way, the way to go, and the way to survive. Now, you are ready to go see Fire Star."

"But … but no! I don't want to!"

"There is no running away. There is only walking forward in Spirit. Come."

She took my hand, and we walked down the trail. My heart was pounding loud in my ears, but my feet gave no resistance to the walking. I could still feel the energy rising up into me from Mother Earth, and, somehow right then, I felt no fear at all.

On our way, a man came toward us, stopping on the trail. He was carrying a dead and partially skinned animal. I remembered Gun introducing me to him at the first ceremony. Singing Brook stopped, looked at the animal, and was impressed. He offered her a piece of the meat to eat, and she took it and ate it without hesitation. I was appalled.

When the man offered me some, I must have leapt back three feet. "Are you kidding? Why would I do that?"

"This is the way to honor the animal you eat," he told me. "You thank it for its flesh and then you eat it while it is still warm from the beat of its own heart and the racing of its own blood. Now the life force of the animal joins yours."

I frowned. "How cruel."

"Isn't it more cruel to deny the animal conscious movement into your flesh … to eat the animal body long after its spirit has left it? That body of yours really only eats to feed your spirit. You might as well learn that now, 'cuz someday you won't have one … a body I mean. Here, have a bite."

He held the bleeding meat to my mouth. I clamped my lips tightly shut.

He looked irritated. "Maybe your prefer the delicacy of the still-beating heart. Shall I cut it out?"

Singing Brook said, "No. What you offer is fine for now." She turned to me. "It will be a good thing for you. Warrior energy. A good thing for you now."

"Have a bite." He pushed the meat to my lips.

"Not that way," Brook stopped him. "Here." She took the flesh from him and prayed over it. Then she held it with her two hands, high into the air, as if offering it to the sky. Next she bowed and came up offering it to me.

For some reason, I was deeply touched by her respect for spirit and for me, so I accepted the flesh into my mouth from her fingers – but then almost spit it out. She put two fingers gently over my mouth. "Don't spit. Swallow. You need to know the warrior."

For sister Singing Brook, I did this. Then she repeated something several times in what I figured was Tslagee. I felt a crystalline exhilaration trickle through me.

I must have been starving for nutrition, because just then a bolt of strength raced into my every cell.

part three:

heart knows

11.
on the path

Singing Brook and I walked on down the path.

The sun was bright. I felt a calmness emerge within me. When Fire Star appeared out of the blue, suddenly standing in a small clearing, alone, I was not surprised. We stopped, faced him, and said nothing. He looked at Singing Brook. "Leave us," he commanded.

"No," was all she said.

"Leave us," he narrowed his eyes at her.

Singing Brook held steady. "Not without your word."

"She is my woman."

I started to argue the point but Singing Brook silenced me with a subtle touch of her hand. "If this is so, she can divorce you at any time. Our women can always make this decision. Shouldn't she know this?"

"There are times when this is not the way it is. And she is not blood."

"I see you are mixing up the old ways with whatever stories you want to tell to make your flawed plan work."

"You see very little, woman," he told her as his eyes bored into her head.

Singing Brook looked at Fire Star sternly, as if he were a bad boy. "Say you will make no demands of her flesh."

Fire Star glared harder at Singing Brook and narrowed his eyes even more. She looked right back at him unusually calmly. He amped up his glare further. Brook amped up her unusual calm further. Fire Star amped his glare again, and then, at its peak, abruptly backed down. "Right. Then I will not take her against her wish."

Singing Brook touched my hand again, whispered in my ear something only I could hear, "*Maka Shan*," and then walked off. I was startled by her comment, and disturbed by her departure. I didn't want her to leave, but I couldn't figure out a respectable way for me to ask her to stay.

Once Singing Brook was out of sight, Fire Star looked at me coldly. "Spirit tells me you carry my child."

An alarm went off deep inside me. What? "No I do not."

He looked at me surprised. Then he collected himself. "You may not know yet, but you do."

"You're wrong."

Fire Star's face softened for just a moment. "Why do you rebel? You have the honor of carrying my child. And you have the chance to become my closest apprentice, if you can follow the path. It is not usual for a man to offer such teachings to a woman."

I wanted to cry, but I didn't. I wanted things to be different. I wanted him to be the man I had believed him to be. "Before I met you,

I admired you so much. I believed in you and what you were saying to people. You told about the future of the Earth. And you said that power can be a quiet thing. I loved that. I still believe your teachings, because they are bigger than you. But I don't want you for my teacher. Not anymore."

He remained softened, but barely. "Why would you change now that you carry my child?"

Now I had to force my words out of my tightening mouth. "I said I don't carry your child. Anyway, I changed because of what you did to me."

"You should thank me, woman. I initiated you into the Tribe."

"Oh no you didn't. You took my body for your own use and under false pretences. For sure I don't thank you."

"No. You are wrong. Spirit took us both for bigger design. We were but in service to spirit."

"You can't dress it up with all that talk. I was there. I know what happened. I will always remember what happened."

His face became stone-like, with his eyes transmitting a look I had never before seen. "I have had a vision. Your are honored with my child. But, you will try something—"

"I don't know what you're talking about."

"You should know that you will not leave here with my child."

"I am a free person."

"Not when you are with a man's child."

"I don't have your child."

"If you kill my child, you die, too. We have ways to be sure of this."

"You are a terrible man. People should know that you are not a great leader. You don't even respect your own old ways."

He grabbed me, twisted my wrist as if to break it, and then held it that way as he moved to my back. He put his other hand on my abdomen and chanted. After a while, his hold on my arm loosened and both his arms were around me, locked in a kind of embrace as he stood still behind me. He relaxed and became a bit gentle. "Sweet goddess, my sweet young woman, we will name you next time. You will be happy soon. We will marry."

"Let me go. I don't want you. I don't want your naming. I don't want your guides to mark me. I don't want the name your guides give me to follow me through my life. My guides say I am Akashakana."

"Guides, hah. You do not know the sacred way of medicine guides." Fire Star's embrace tightened harshly.

"Yes I do," I said boldly, hearing my own resolution with surprise.

I dug my nails deep into Fire Star's arms and he flinched. I threw his hands off and stepped away, turning around to let him know my stand. "Don't ever touch me again."

I turned to march off, but he grabbed my hand. "You carry a man's son; you are that man's vessel. You are mine, so you will grow to love me."

"What makes you think that even if I were pregnant, I would have a son? It could be a daughter."

"No, the son is born to grow and take the chief's place."

"A girl can take the chief's place."

Fire Star began to laugh wildly. "A girl?"

While he was laughing, I figured I would have the last word. "Well, it doesn't matter because I'm not having your baby! That's crazy!" and I ran off, away from him, on down the trail. When I looked back, he was walking in the other direction. I felt sad and confused.

I half-ran for a few more minutes – then felt a new kind of deep tiredness in my body, an exhaustion carried through ages and eons into that time – into our times. I went off the trail a few yards into the woods, where I sank down to the ground, almost into it. *Maka, Maka,* this was Earth, Mother Earth, Maka Maka Maka Shan. I didn't do any thinking, my stunned mind was a blank. I just laid there. At first I wasn't aware of much of anything at all. I was only relieved to have gotten away from Fire Star without being further harmed. The talk about a child inside me made no sense then, I couldn't feel any hint that I was pregnant. And I certainly didn't want to feel that hint.

This time immersed in nature consoled me. This passage in time manifested its own special spirit. Each passing minute came alive and was its own compassionate existence, its own caress full of the comfort and love I longed for. Living, breathing, being, time….

Time.

Time.

I began to hear sounds in great detail, nature sounds, all around me. I could hear my own breaths coming and going, feel my own body living – and also feel the air, the woods, the birds and animals around me. The breeze was sighing way up in the tops of the tall trees. I looked up, and caught a flash of sunlight gleaming through the green boughs, and a white cloud shape-shifting overhead. Now, a strange sense of waiting suspense, suspended suspense, came over me. It seemed a message was about to be handed to me by someone invisible.

But just then I heard voices nearby, and my body jumped up to greet them. Something in me wanted very much, right then, to be with other human beings, not to be alone any longer. I didn't want the invisible messenger to find me.

A man they would call a red man, and a woman they would call a white woman, were coming up the trail. I stepped out rather timidly to greet them.

"Hi," the small, very pale woman said. "You're the girl who wouldn't be named. I'm Flower, this is Tree Dog. What are you called anyway?"

"I got called Lilith a lot," I said. "Now I guess it's Akashakana."

"We're headed to pipe ceremony," the man said. He had feathers hanging from the back of his long braided hair and was carrying several long sticks. "Come."

"Well, I don't know, I—"

"You can't have anything better to do," Flower laughed sweetly. "So come on. You'll like it, Akashakana."

I shrugged and followed them five minutes along the path to where an outdoor ceremony was being conducted in a large circle, in what I would later be told was three different native tongues. I wasn't sure if I belonged enough to participate, but Flower wanted me to sit right in the circle where she and her friend were taking their places. So, after checking to be sure Fire Star was nowhere in sight, I sat with them.

I felt out of place. A couple of people frowned at my intrusion and I started to leave, but Tree Dog put his hand on my leg, insisting that I not move. The ceremony was in progress. A flute-like tobacco pipe was held up to the sky and pointed in the four directions of the compass. Then it was passed. Eventually it came to me.

I was nervous, concerned that I would make a wrong move and offend these serious people. After all, what could I know about the sacred, I asked myself. I tried to look like I knew what I was doing. I mimicked the procedure of receiving the pipe and turning it around 360 degrees before pointing it in the four compass directions, then mumbling something under my breath, then smoking a little, and then passing it on to the next person in a certain way.

The ceremony began to deepen my feelings, and I quickly grew to understand it well, as if I had known it all along. I began to feel a little more part of it all. I moved into a certain form of peaceful, timeless, prayer-trance state, one I thought I had never known before. After perhaps half an hour, amidst all the singing and chanting and praying of all the people around me, I felt a light tap on my shoulder. I turned my head just a bit, trying not to disrupt the ceremony by looking away.

No one was there. I turned back to the ceremony.

But then there was another tap. I looked back again, and for just a moment, out of the corner of my eye, I thought I saw an old woman wearing a long robe standing there looking at me. My eyes opened really big, as if I'd seen a ghost. Just as I realized that this was the image of Sveeka, the same old woman – ghost of my mother I'd seen several times now, she disappeared. Poof! Was that a baby she was carrying away?

Astonished and feeling suddenly deeply forlorn, I turned back to the ceremony. Fortunately, I told myself, everyone is praying and has his or her eyes closed, and no one saw me look away from the center. I turned a little, one more time, hoping that the spirit world version of my mother would come back, but no, Sveeka was gone. As I faced the center of the ceremony again, a grandmother sitting across from me caught my eye and nodded a yes. I knew, from her eyes, that she had seen Sveeka, too.

12.
earth changes

Time flowed on.

The days and nights that followed were, for me, a series of usually very subtle but nevertheless progressively profound unveilings. Up there, in that isolated and unique place, the wall between the day world and the spirit realm seemed worn precipitously yet beautifully thin. This was a time when, with each passing moment, my appreciation of not only nature but of the cosmos expanded. I could feel myself opening to a new understanding of everything.

I did struggle with the trauma that accompanied my initiation into this amazing world. This trauma, brought on when the self proclaimed medicine man compelled me to have sex with him, stayed with me. I just couldn't shake it. But time went on, and in a gentle way, time itself soothed me.

In further conversations, Singing Brook explained, "The people here live close in to the spirit realm. All the age-old native rituals of the various First Tribes that we merge and practice here are aimed at keeping the door to and from the spirit realm open. This lets the ones who are really strict about the practices be in continuous contact with the spirits of the dead and of the living. It lets them communicate with the Earth herself, with Maka, something people who are going to truly navigate the coming Earth changes must know how to do. It also lets them traverse the realms, back and forth, at will."

Earth changes. Earth changes. The phrase resonated through me. Something about what Singing Brook was teaching me made sense. I could feel the logic feeding my soul. Once in a while, I tried to speak to Singing Brook about the matter of "*Maka Shan*" and what I was coming to just feel was the Wazine way. All she would tell me was that I knew far more than she -- and that I should be telling her....

I could not understand why she thought this about me....

It was clear to me that I couldn't leave this place, at least not for the present moment. The Chief, Fire Star, had made it clear to everyone that I could not be let out. And, as I met more people and felt more a part of this world, I surrendered some of my urgency to get away – at least for a while. Fire Star was now leaving me mostly alone and was often gone. Usually when he came up to this piece of tribal land, he stayed with the men, or a few older women with whom he also shared council. He led a few ceremonies for the whole community.

Once in a while, however, Fire Star would show up and demand a private meeting with me. Each time he met with me, he let me know that he was in charge of my fate. He implied that, at his wish, I could be dead. And also that, at his wish, I was eligible to partake of the most rare and sacred wisdom he shared with only a few. What a shocking choice.

Sometimes he would call me to a large boulder. First, he and I would have a stiff nonverbal standoff. Then he would let me know he wanted me again. I would then say, "Never." He would then say, "You are mine, my woman." My answer was always "No." His was always, "The baby is a boy." Again and again I insisted, "There is no baby and even if there were, it would be a girl."

He would laugh at this. "Never a girl to do this job."

"I don't know what job you're talking about," I told him every time we talked.

"To lead this new Tribe and to lead all the people, whatever tribe they are, through." He kept saying this.

"Through what?"

"The Earth changes. *Maka, Maka Shan.* You do know, my beautiful young priestess, you do know about the coming changes. This will be the Maka's Shan. We know you know, more than you know you know. But you do know. Listen to yourself, listen well."

Moments like this, when he would tell me this, waves of chills would race through my veins. But I would always try to wall his message out: "Don't expect me to listen to what you have to say. I have no respect for you now. You killed that respect."

"Respect is bigger than we are. My beautiful white spirit, you are here for the truth, whether you want it or not."

I would shake my head no, every time he told me. But I would somehow hear what he had to say anyway. *Maka Shan?*

"This is important. Time will tell you that our meeting matters. Talk to the Earth, woman. Talk to Mother Earth, *Maka*."

I would stand there belligerently, saying nothing aloud. But, each time we talked, my curiosity would be peaked. It would be shocked into higher interest each time. And, I would then say something to the Earth very quietly and secretly in my mind. To my continuous amazement, which I would always struggle to conceal, the Earth would always answer. A language would speak itself into my head by way of my feet, up through my torso, into my heart where it grew loud and pulsated and then moved into my mind. I would shudder a little.

Fire Star would see this. "You see again. You see you feel the energy of the Earth. You also feel the energy of my seed. Let me give you more of my seed, right here, right now."

"No."

"Woman, I can take you if I want to. I want you."

"No."

"Akashakana, I love you."

"No, you don't."

"In my way, I do."

"No."

"Well, you will see my way soon enough. For now then, just hear the Earth. You will see more and more in your life, you hear the voice of the planet. You do. This is a gift. You are among those chosen to hear her. This is not a job you can say no to. You are here for Maka, Maka Shan. ... I can help you with all this. Let me."

Torn in two directions, I would glower at Fire Star. Why would such a repulsive animal be here to teach me what I was so very very driven to learn?

He would always tell me, "Woman, you pain me. But, you do not have to like the messenger to need to know the message. And you know you have been called to hear it. You know."

Called.

A calling was making its way into my spirit. Or better stated, this calling was revealing itself to me from within and without my spirit. Maka was talking, right?

13.
maka shan

Time still moved me on its river.

I tried to make sense of how I had come to be there on that tribal land, to ask myself if I truly had come to learn something – to receive some kind of message. I tried to think in the way I always had, but I found that my way of thinking was changing. Information was coming to me in another way. And I was processing it differently. ... Whether this was truly information rather than merely stories calling me, I was being swept into it. It would be a long time before I would see how much information can even be carried in stories and myths, and in religions as well.

I felt myself to be suspended in a kind of still motion. This sacred land caught me in its energy and then held my attention. Despite my resistance, I found something special happening. For the first time, I really lived in this world. I was really connected to life on this Earth. *Maka*, Earth, had became my teacher. She cradled me and comforted me in my confusion. The *skhan* or motion -- the motion formed from the *skan* and the *shan* of the wind, the *tateh* -- became so much more to me than what we think of as wind. Moving air was alive. *Skhan tateh* was a living thing, a spirit who I came to know on a personal basis. Even the *inyan*, the stones, were alive. And the *ksa*, the goddess of water – she nourished me every time I took a sip of this *mini*, or water.

Tateh Skhan, Maka Shan. Tateh Skhan, Maka Shan. Tateh Skhan, Maka Shan.

I grew to accept my unusual state of mind and heightened sensitivity. The spirits were all around me. I did not question their distinct existence. The sky was open like a doorway. I proceeded to move into a state of subtle surrender and to bask in this semi-ascended environment, although I certainly was not able to know what this semi-ascended state might mean or was about. Not back then. It would take years to get it, or maybe to increasingly know it. And that calling would grow louder and louder, even when I tried not to hear.

I started to feel that the worst was over, and the best yet to come. And I admit – I was intrigued. I was entranced. I had spent so much of my young life hoping and trying to contact at will the space beyond the material world. I had been searching for an opening as long as I could remember. The modern ever more hi-tech white world had never made a place for my visions, yet this humble tribal land place had. The white world had cruelly walled out my perceptions of a possibly ascended, inter-dimensional, reality. However, this place of the Tribe had encouraged them, almost demanded them.

And, deep down in my soul, I had always instinctively wanted to go home – back to the stars. Like Kiowa, I wanted to be able to come and go at will. So I decided that as long as I was stuck there on tribal land, I should learn as much as I could about how I might travel back to the stars. There was no longer any question – I could feel the spirits walking among us. I could feel them brushing against me. When the wind blew, I felt the cool rush of wings. In my dreams, I learned to ignite a white flight within me. I learned to truly fly. And I came to know myself well as Akashakana. Who I was was becoming. Where the name might be shifting and would shift again and again in my life, the meaning of the naming would stay with me.

Missing him, I naturally wanted to know where Kiowa had gone. I asked Tree Dog and he told me that Kiowa was a wanderer and that he was a fugitive. With Gun's friends' help, Kiowa had escaped from a military mental hospital where they had put him for seeing spirits come for the dead and dying in the battlefield trenches of the Viet Nam War. Now Kiowa lived off the Earth and he came and went at will from higher into the mountains and even from places in the sky.

I asked Singing Brook where Kiowa went and she raised her eyebrows. "Hmmm," she teased, "I can hear your heart beat calling him."

"No, it's not like that," I told her. But maybe it was, in part, like that.

Singing Brook said, "He will come when you truly call him."

"But how can I call him?"

"You will find a real way. Through your real heart."

I tried and tried, with no luck. Kiowa didn't come. Where had he gone? Back into the sky? Home? Without me? I kept trying to figure out how to call Kiowa.

Then, after three months of insight and learning in what had come to feel like a strange but second home for me, a harsh day came. I had to admit to myself I was indeed pregnant. It certainly was not Mark's baby. I had not, in the past months, had even the modified sex with no penetration and no risk of pregnancy that I had been having with Mark before he left to join the Tribe. I hadn't wanted to be close to any man since – since that night – with Fire Star.

As some young women still in the throes of adolescence are still prone to do, I waited, thinking the problem would just go away. I would wake up one day and not be pregnant. But no – nothing went away. So I finally told Mark. I still remember his reaction. He and tall skinny Jim, the only other eighteen year olds living there on the land, came in to the old barn where I had been sitting alone for most of the day. The three of us had become a sort of team.

"Hi," Jim patted me on the head. "Been lookin' for ya' girl."

"Hi, Jim. Mark, I'm pregnant."

Jim sighed loudly, sat down facing out the doorway, and muttered, "Oh boy. Here we go, man."

Mark was silent for a while. "It can't be mine." He hung his head.

"That's what I'm trying to say. It's his." I shivered, cold to the bone. "He's the only person I've been with in Seven months – since you."

"You sure?"

"There's been no one else even near. It took me months to believe you were really going to be staying with these people and you really wanted me to quit college and lose my scholarship and give up my life and come to you. Finally I came – to that gateway house in Sacramento – he did it to me there. And you and I haven't been together that way, any way, since I got here. And now I've been here at this place three and a half months."

Mark looked at me blankly. I could tell that, somehow, he wasn't surprised. "I didn't want to tell you," he said. "People around here've been saying that you're pregnant with Fire Star's baby ... and that the baby, well, that it's the next generation's chief ... the leader through the coming Earth changes, and or the world revolution, whichever comes first."

It would be years later I would realize that this next generation's chief would come in no matter what happened up there with this tribe.

Jim stood up and leaned on the side of the doorway. "Fire Star knows. That's what they tell me."

"Mark, I have to do something," I blurted out.

"What?"

I'd already made up my mind – there somehow wasn't even a question about it deep inside me. "An abortion."

"Oh boy," Jim sighed again. "I'm getting out'a here." He went out the door and scooted away.

Mark was quiet for a long time. Then he took a deep breath. "Why don't you keep it? It'll be okay with me."

I was astonished. "What are you saying?"

"They say the spirits have willed this. You've got to keep it."

"Why do you say that? It's a rape baby, Mark. A rape baby can be aborted. That's not wrong. They have to let me out to get an abortion."

Mark seemed to turn to stone. He seemed to be offended by what I had said, by the fact that I was critical of Fire Star – and had called that man's baby a rape baby.

Mark reached over, put his hand on mine, and said, "Well, what I feel is that the baby is Creator's baby, and this is a good thing. Can't you see that?"

I couldn't see that. I put his hand off me, stood up and walked out of the building and down the path, fuming with my own emotions, my reaction to being let down by Mark. All I could think was that I had to get away from all this. And if I couldn't find an easier way soon, I would walk out – thirty miles or whatever – to the road, at night if I had to.

But that was a stupid idea.

Isn't it interesting how much easier it is to see things when looking back on them much later....

14.
captive liberation

The days passed.

The weeks passed. No Kiowa. No way out. Mark and Jim kept begging me to stay. They were afraid of what would happen to me if I tried to leave. They told me they had heard I would be killed. Or just die.

Life with the Tribe began to change for me, as I started to see that it had an intensely unreal quality to it. I began to feel very strongly that we were all stuck. We were trapped on an ideological island, an island waiting for the rest of the world to have what the Tribe thought would be a major cataclysm. My perceptions of the entire situation took on new dimensions. This was a crazy Tribe, I now found myself thinking – a band of dreamers waiting for an overturn of modern day reality and a subsequent utopia to just happen to them.

Whatever protected "teachings" were being protected there, they were being rather misunderstood. It's not that this material wasn't respected, as it was. But I could not help but feel that this Chief was using these teachings for his own self-serving purpose. Or maybe he was being influenced by forces larger than he was. Or maybe he was quite confused. All this stuff was very hard to know.

And many people here didn't seem to want to – or maybe to be able to – think logically. The Tribe's founding dream was wonderful, but the implementation of it was becoming, at least in my eyes, a nightmare.

I tried several times to share my feelings with some of them, to reason with them, to add a new perspective. But in response, they treated me more and more as an outcast. People there seemed to be mesmerized by Fire Star and the purpose of the Tribe. Anything said in even slight disagreement with Fire Star was sacrilege, especially if it came from me, who carried his child. Anything said by me was viewed as complete disagreement with the sacred Earth change teachings. But they were wrong about my views. I just could not help but question the intentions of Fire Star.

Most of the time I was the only one who now and then dared to openly stand up against Fire Star's orders and ideas.

The more I wanted out, the more urgent the idea of getting my abortion became, the more I realized I was genuinely trapped. I waited and waited and waited, praying for release. And my sense of being trapped became an out-and-out feeling of living in captivity. I grew to feel I was being held captive in a crazy community where true visions were turned into dishonest excuses for tyranny, and sacred old teachings were reinterpreted as profane excuses for abuse. For my part, I didn't know whether it was more dangerous to try to leave, or to stay. So there I was, sitting in limbo. I sat and I waited for an answer, and I waited for Kiowa, since I still felt that he was my guide.

While I waited, despite my rebellion against Fire Star and his leadership, and even though I was pregnant and not wanting to be, I continued to regularly catch myself experiencing great joy, profound beauty, and profound insight. Step by step, I began to absorb, right into my core, certain deep ancient teachings that would only fully unfold within my consciousness decades later. These would later resurface when I was deep into another world, deep into a career, deep into a long marriage and then subsequent divorce, and -- deep into leaving this Tribe experience and its teachings so very far behind. *(But this is a story for later Maka Shan Saga volumes. Stay tuned.)*

And one thing I learned from the old woman, Wei-shannah, who had seen me see my mother's ghost, Sveeka, during that first pipe ceremony, was how to call someone to me. It took great focus and pure connection between myself and the essence of who I was calling. It was like establishing an excellent telephone connection and then drawing the person on the other end of the line to me. Wei-shannah told me, "You can do this with the living or the dead, with humans or star people, but it will take many years of practice to perfect your ability. But you are one who can and should."

For over a month, something inside me chose not to try this refined technique to call Kiowa. The time never felt right – I couldn't focus in his direction. Then, one morning, I suddenly felt ready. I called him to me – I felt him near me – I touched his essence. I felt him approaching, dissolving into the space I was in. The very next day, close to sunset, while I was walking through the woods, Kiowa appeared before me, stepping causally out from behind a tree.

"Kiowa!" I hugged him and started to cry. I didn't mind showing him my tears. "Oh my God, Creator, thank you, you're back!"

He touched my slightly rounded belly and looked at me knowingly. "I heard you calling. You see, you are learning the ways."

I was bursting with urgency. "Kiowa, I've got to leave here. You have to take me out of here. You have to."

"I came on foot."

"Then I'll hike out with you."

"Cannot take you where I'm going. It's deeper into the mountains." He looked up at the sky. "No place for a young woman."

"Please, Kiowa. Please. Help me get out. I have to do something about this." I pointed to my belly. "I don't want to have his baby."

Kiowa seemed to know I was pregnant. And I was beginning to show. "There is nothing to be done. Creator will decide this dispute."

"Dispute?"

"You are disagreeing with the creation of life. This is not something I can help with. I am just a humble servant of Creator. I do not serve as an instrument for the destruction of life. But I can help you see how you can guide this life to the best place."

"I really don't know what you're talking about."

166

"Sit. You can think about how this life that is with you will exist in the same way no matter what you do or think. Your choices are not yours and it will not be you making them even when you feel you are. You will know all you need to know. ... This life was here before, waiting for the right time to come in. If this time is not right, this life will know and make this choice."

I sat. We watched as the sun moved to go down.

I was frustrated with my dear beloved Kiowa, my guide, my friend. Why wouldn't anyone help me? "I don't see any wisdom in doing nothing about this," I told him.

In response, Kiowa closed his eyes. I watched him as he fingered the small white leather medicine bag, beaded with blue and ivory beads, which hung around his neck. As he did so, he began to sing. His voice moaned and curled around his exotic tones, but, so far as I know, none of his sounds were words in any language. There were mostly *hey's* and *yoh's*. His voice carried this ancient lament through the sundown into the night.

For a while, I was restless. And then I succumbed, mesmerized by the chant. Now I could repeat the sounds and the melody. I began to sing along. I seemed to know this star song. I remembered it somehow. He reached over and put my hands on my belly and held them there until we stopped singing. By then the night sky was bringing in the stars.

"Kiowa, those stars out there, they're where I'm from."

"What makes you think this spirit you carry does not come from the stars like you?" Kiowa asked quietly as he took my hands and pressed them into my belly.

A little spark seemed to fly into my hands from deep within my womb. I had forgotten my hands were there on my belly. I jolted a bit and looked down at my abdomen. It seemed to be giving off some light. I blinked hard and looked again.

"What's that you see?" Kiowa asked.

"Is that the life?"

"Ask it."

"Are you the life?"

The light grew brighter and more expansive. "Oh, wow ... look," I whispered. "It's so beautiful ... magical. So amazing."

"And I cherish that light, that life. Can you see why I cannot help you put that light out?"

I didn't want to, but I couldn't help but see. A spasm of anguish hit me. "But what should I do, Kiowa? What should I do?" A few tears slipped down my cheeks.

"Try communing with the spirit who has come to grow within you. Speak to this spirit. You are so close together, you might as well speak to each other."

"What should I say?"

"What do you feel moved to say?"

"That I can't do this right now. That love was not part of the equation. That I am too young and too confused. That these people are holding me prisoner."

"That kind of communication is too muddled for a clear spirit new to this place. Your emotions will not get your message there." Kiowa looked at me and saw that I still had no idea what to do. So he reached over and swirled his hands around me. The world around us felt him.

A syrupy wind was summoned. It was heavy, heavy air. I could do nothing but lay down. I felt as if I were slipping through a hole in the ground. What I lay on didn't seem solid like the ground. What was I slipping into? Falling, falling, falling. Deeper. Now I was groggy. I felt a bit of surprise but mostly fascination. "Where am I going Kiowa?" I tried to say clearly but couldn't. "How are you doing this?" I murmured.

"In," was all he said.

And next I knew, I was there inside my womb, with the fetus! And, being there, a rapture the likes of which I had never imagined I would feel swept over me. I stayed there in that bliss for a forever or two. I was sublimely happy there. Infinite bliss. And then I heard Kiowa clap lightly.

I came back. I lay there with my eyes closed, not wanting to be back. "Hey, what'd you do that for, Kiowa?"

"It is not good to stay in too long. You may not be able to return."

"That would've been all right with me."

"Well, if you had not come back you would have killed your baby by dying."

"Killed my baby?" Now the thought repulsed me. I had touched the gift of life. I had been one with the bliss of Creation.

So now I was torn. Ripped in two. "Kiowa," I moaned, "I am of split heart."

"Well then, Akashakana, your split heart must heal."

Here Kiowa had proposed the impossible so far as I was concerned. "Yeah, but how do I do that?"

"Wait. And wait. And wait more. And listen more. Listen. The answers are there if you listen. Feel the spirit in your head."

I frowned and was about to object. Kiowa reached over and put a finger to my lips to silence me. I wanted to cry, I felt so torn. But Kiowa wanted to go on. "Give it the time it wants. Use the rising energy of the split force to heal. Wait. Listen to the energy rise. When the time comes to solve the split, the energy of the split will help you."

I was trying to follow him. He went on, concentrating hard on getting through to me. "You hear me now; you will know what I have said later. It works that way. Always when you wait and listen, the answers, the resolutions, they come. And then," he touched my cheek, "and then, Akashakana, sometimes things happen for you. Things you cannot decide to do for yourself. Someone else, another spirit, reaches in. Like a parent pulling a tooth out for a frightened child. Or a chain of events takes over."

I saw Kiowa lift, and then mumble something to his small white leather medicine bag. He saw me see. "My prayer medicine. Always with me. Like my heart."

We heard a rustle. "Come, follow me," Kiowa leapt up and extended his hand.

I grabbed his hand and followed, tripping and then swearing under my breath about my clumsiness.

Kiowa turned and stopped me. "Shhh. Walk softly. Walk with no sound." He went on ahead and I followed. He turned and stopped me again. "I said walk softly. No sound."

"I am."

"Not like this," Kiowa said as he pretended he was stomping his foot. "Like this," he whispered as he rolled his foot, toe first, onto the ground in slow motion, producing absolutely no noise. And then he lifted his foot in reverse way.

"Why?" I whispered as I followed him again, this time mimicking his steps as best I could.

"Because you are spirit stalking."

"Spirit stalking?"

"Yes, being one with the Earth and the spirit of the animal you follow. The Earth will talk to you and tell you where to step. This is how you will always know where to go … and how to stalk … and also know when you're being stalked."

"Oh." I tried the silent step.

"Good. Now move more slowly, so slowly that you feel you are still."

I tried a few steps.

"That's right, move still. Still is a big thing. It is a whole sensation. It is the highest form of motion. It is when *like rushing water nothing moves*," he whispered.

Now we moved soundlessly and ever so slowly into the now night forest. I even kept my breaths long and slow and quiet. I was watching the ground so closely that I failed to realize that we were standing amidst a heard of wild deer. Only when Kiowa stopped moving completely and I mimicked him by freezing, did I look up.

"Hah, look at that!" I shouted. And all the deer ran away. Poof!

Kiowa whirled back to me, at first looking very stern, and then, seeing my bewilderment, falling to the ground laughing. At first I was insulted to have him laughing at me, but after a while I caught the mirth, as if it was contagious. I sat down and had the best and perhaps only real laugh I had had since before my mother had died.

Suddenly, Kiowa said, "Quiet. Look."

He pointed a few feet away. A huge-eyed fawn stared at us, and behind her, clustered in the trees, was the herd. We sat there in silence and let them look at us a while. "They stalk us, so be still." Kiowa put his arm around me and held me close to him for a long time, to keep me still.

After a long while, the deer grew bored of us and wandered away. Kiowa's arm was still tight around me. I noticed I liked the feeling.

"Kiowa," I whispered, still staring straight ahead.

"Yes?"

We turned our faces to each other, not thinking about how close we already were, and our lips touched by accident. That's all, just touched. Not kissed.

I think we stayed still – just like that – a long time. In that perfect time when the whole world spun around just the two of us and harmony rang, I knew I had fallen in love for the first time in my life. Eventually, I pulled just far enough away to say something, something silly: "Kiowa, I love you."

He touched me, his left hand above my heart – and he put my left hand above his heart. We were silent like this as we studied each other's eyes. He held my gaze while his face shape shifted -- from old, old man to young, young boy to a Kiowa of many different ages -- with an owl face and then a wolf face flickering in between his faces at different ages. When the shifting of faces slowed, I saw a regal condor in the skin of his face.

"You … what is this I see … a condor eagle man?"

"And I see you … the phoenix dove woman."

"Kiowa, I see the bird right in your face."

"Dove, condor, phoenix," he murmured.

"I love you more than I can ever find a way to say," I told him.

"And I love you, but—" He stopped and sunk his face into his two hands for several minutes. I was wondering if he was about to cry when he finally told me, "This is wrong. What we love is Creator's light coming to us through each other."

"Well, that might be true, Kiowa, but I love you as well as Creator."

"But you are a white woman," Kiowa moaned.

"So? … If that's so, then does this mean you're repulsed by me? Anyway, I am many colors, you know that." I was faintly insulted.

"No. I love you. Sure as I can be, I do. But, I cannot marry out of my tribe."

I was thrilled. "We're not so far as marriage yet. Just love."

"Well, I am making you my half side in my mind already. That's like a wife. I must stop. I am wanting you already. I must stop."

I leaned closer in to him with a surge of youthful and naïve persistence. He put his hands on either side of my face to push me away, and he started to push me away. But instead he abruptly switched directions and pulled me to him. His kiss was long and passionate, warm and exciting, but it ended abruptly. "We must stop, woman."

"Well, at least you call me 'woman.' "

We kissed again. He pulled me down and lay next to me. Then he pulled me on top of him and hugged me tight. Then he rolled very gently up over me, and then back off, seeming to wrestle with himself.

He sat up. "I know you haven't yet touched the real wonders of real love between a man and a woman."

I sat up and started to protest his conclusion, as I didn't want to seem too inexperienced. He shook his head no quickly, put a finger to my lips and whispered, "You deserve to be made love to and not violated. I should love you the right way. No I should not. I should."

I blinked and stared at him. What was he saying? Then he seemed to disapprove of himself for saying whatever he'd just said and went on, "But this is not my way. I cannot have you. I pledged my ancestors never to marry outside my Earth tribe."

I was so wistful I thought I would wilt. "Everyone around here seems to think mixing tribes and races is what's supposed to happen."

"I for one do not break the ancient tradition."

"Times are changing though," I said meekly.

"Yes. Times are changing." He put one palm to the Earth and one on his forehead. "Time will open soon: we near the end of this time. You will know this more, later in your life. You have come to help forge the needed rebalancing, the Great Return."

He pulled me to him and kissed me wildly.

Abruptly, he pushed me away, seeming to wrestle with himself yet again. "No, you are someone else's woman. And you are here on a mission."

"No, I am not here on a mission. And, anyway, no, I am my own woman. I am not Mark's."

"I was not speaking of Mark. You carry another man's child."

"Well, you can't possibly mean I belong to that false medicine man, Fire Star?"

"When you carry a man's offspring, your womb becomes his property."

"You can't mean that. Not you of all people."

"It is then your responsibility to bring in that child, to bear his child, the product of his seed. Or to let the child decide the path."

"That is weird. There's some kind of conflict in your way of thinking, Kiowa. You want me to be my own woman."

"Well, yes. And you are, and you will be more and more, until you are yourself a leader, but not right now. Some traditions do make the woman or at least her womb the man's property while she carries his child, especially if he is a chief."

"I don't think he's a chief. But, whatever is true about him, it's my child."

"You have told his people you don't even want to give birth to the baby. Doesn't it make sense he would want to protect the life of his fertilized seed ... his family line? Especially since all visions say you are the one—"

"Oh please, not this again. The ONE WHAT, for God's, Creator's, sakes?"

Kiowa stared at my face and then, as if noticing it for the first time, ran his finger over my right cheekbone. He raised his eyebrows. "The one to bring in the new leader. For the new world."

I moaned and shook my head no. I couldn't accept that even Kiowa had been so ideologically compromised, brainwashed. But then, I myself was struggling with that state of mind.

Kiowa stood up. So did I. "We must go back now," he insisted.

"But Kiowa—"

"Come, woman," he smiled and put his arm around me. He held me tight. "I promise I will pray to Creator for the Truth about you." He started to walk and pulled me with him. "I will go deep into the mountains and ask: Is she the one? Is she the sign we have been waiting for? Must I stay away and not tarnish this medicine priestess with the longings of my heart, of my manhood?"

He looked up at the stars and started to shout, as if demanding an answer, "Or is she the one you promised me? Is she the white buffalo woman returned from the stars ... from the same tribe of star ancestors ... the one you promised would be sent to me, if I stayed here?"

At first, I thought he was being dramatic. Then I looked at his face and saw a tear, just one tear, on one cheek, as he listened to something I could not hear. He then began to wail, "Must I let this woman I have come to love ... to want ... to long for -- Must I let my star sister, my love, go?"

He fell to his knees and hugged my legs. I was quite taken aback by this show of adoration and desperation. I didn't know what to do. I was too young to feel this sort of passion. But I was crying.

Finally he stood up. He was resolute.

"What should we do, Kiowa?" I whispered.

"Creator will tell us. I will wait for a sign and then we will see."

"That's fine ... to listen to Creator ... but this is something for us to decide, not...."

"No. This is a question for the highest high Council, the elder of elders, Creator. There is no real marriage without Creator's blessing. When you have Creator's blessing, you know it, you just know it. All else that we would call love is fool's gold. Don't throw yourself away for fool's gold."

"Oh, I won't. But being with you is not throwing myself away. Our love is not fool's gold."

"You are so beautiful, so sweet. I could spend a lifetime with you, I could. But maybe this is not the path we are to follow here. You see, you must accept the power."

"What power?"

"The powered transferred."

"What?"

"The unwitting and unwilling, but absolutely irrevocable, transfer that takes place when a medicine man forces himself upon a wo --" Kiowa stopped and froze, as if he should not have said whatever he was starting to say.

"What? A woman? Forces himself on a woman? What happens when?"

Kiowa studied my face carefully and smiled softly. "Look, its about power, medicine power. Many try to keep it, some try to protect it, some hoard it. No medicine man wants to lose this power." Kiowa was forcing himself not to say the big truth he knew about all this.

"I can not make any sense out of this, Kiowa." I was agitated, almost struggling not to deal with what I, maybe on some level, was finally hearing.

Kiowa touched my hand. "Look, what I mean to be saying is that it will be many years before you really know."

"Know what?"

"Know what has come to you here with us. What power. What secrets. What this means to who you are. How you were coming into this power one way or another. Back into this power across many lifetimes."

I said nothing. This was too large a knowing for me right then.

Kiowa took my hand and squeezed it. He didn't let go for the rest of that precious night. So precious, each second of that night so precious.

All my life, all the years after this moment, I have felt Kiowa's hand clasping mine. And in that clasp was his firm belief that *when a medicine man rapes a woman, rapes her in any form, his medicine power is transferred to that woman*. Whether that medicine man likes it or not, he is then no longer a true medicine man.

His power was now hers.

15.
blood dawn

It was a long walk back.

In fact, by the time we got back to the camp, it was dawn. We found some kind of ceremonial gathering forming itself. Visitors had arrived. Obviously they'd all hiked in, as I saw backpacks everywhere but absolutely no vehicles. The place was a bustle with preparation. There were more than the usual number of those somber men with guns stomping around in small bands.

We stood off to the side, trying to say something to each other about the precious, exquisitely precious, night we'd just shared. No words came. Instead, I watched the armed men and complained, "Guns again, I hate guns."

"I know how you feel," Kiowa said, "but we really are at war."

"War?"

"Yes, the early time of the New World War – the predicted Great War is now beginning. This war will be taking place on many levels, not just on physical battle fields. It is just beginning. The signs of the emerging Great War are here."

"Great War?"

"It's just beginning, popping up all over the world. It will be many years before this becomes clear. People don't know what this is yet. But they are starting to feel it."

"And so the guns?" I asked.

"It's just that people everywhere, even here, feel it coming. They carry guns, they prepare to someday fight. They feel the revolution but do not understand it yet. Guns, any physical violence, will not be the ultimate force. Watch my words. Decades from now, terrorism will rise to new heights. The world will see. People will struggle to, even fight over the way to, turn the tide."

"Well, I don't understand this, Kiowa."

"Oh yes you do. You will see. World violence, tribal violence, even gender violence, its all about the energies of the Great Rebalancing."

"But Kiowa, whatever this Great Rebalancing thing is, why think we can do it with violence? Why fight to get it done. It will happen anyway, right?"

Kiowa pressed my hand and said, "I have come to love you so deeply. … We have to step back from each other, to be very careful with this energy. … I must drop into the red dawn now … you know, the warrior sweat with the men. I am certain they are aware I have been missing. And maybe missing with you. So it will be a good idea for you to go find Mark."

I started to protest.

"No. You must go now," he whispered sternly, but with very deep and very sad love in his voice, "before we two are an issue around here. Please, dear woman child, go now."

I could see he wasn't going to change his mind. "Okay." I walked off drying the tears as they came to my eyes.

Well, Mark and Jim found me. "Where were you? We thought you got lost."

"On a hike with Kiowa. A sort of vision quest."

"Oh." Mark was a little troubled by this.

"He was teaching me stalking. We got right into the center of a heard of deer."

"That took all night?"

"Mark, leave her alone." Jim jumped in. "Aren't you glad it was Kiowa and that she's okay? It could've been those guys with guns."

"Oh yeah, I guess so."

In the distance, we heard a woman singing like an angel in a native tongue and headed in that direction. We said nothing more to each other.

The Tribe's lead singing woman, Osala, was singing to the Earth and the sky. We all sang with her.

As the sun inched deliberately upward into the blood red sky, the men who had been at the sweat joined the ceremony. They came in like a force – a wave of warriors stepping silently in. I looked at them, trying to understand them as a body, one animal made up of them all. I saw Kiowa. He stood out. He gazed at me. I gazed back. We were so deeply connected now. Fire Star came up next to him. Kiowa held my gaze, but I could feel Fire Star staring at me, trying to pull my gaze to him. I didn't let him. I had fallen completely in love with Kiowa.

Now the ceremony was in full swing. Kiowa and Fire Star moved in next to Osala. I watched the ceremony. A man I didn't know scratched the shape of a human woman into the dirt with a special painted stick. Then another man scratched a large heart into the shape of that woman. The heart had four sections. Osala stopped singing and planted a corn seed in each of the four parts of the woman's heart. The she began to sing her beautiful appeal to the Earth and the sky. One of the men covered each of the four seeds with Earth. The sound of Osala's voice was precise. Every tone seemed to work a bit of magic, as if it were a key to some piece of the universe.

Kiowa caught my eye. He looked up at the sky, his eyes asking me to follow. I looked up at the sky, and lo and behold, there was now but one tiny cloud in the entire sky and it was directly overhead, wearing a brilliant strip of rainbow across itself. I looked back at Kiowa. He nodded upward again. I looked up and now, as clear as could be, the Seven were circling the rainbow. I almost yelped with shock and glee, but knew that I would disturb Osala's work, and controlled myself.

Osala had summoned the Seven priestesses. Did she know about them then?

I looked back at Kiowa. He touched his chest over his heart and then waved his arm to the rainbow and then to me and then put his hand back over his heart. Fire Star caught this and glowered fiercely at

Kiowa, who ignored him. Not wanting anyone else to notice all this between Kiowa and me and Fire Star, I pointed at the sky, gasped, and everyone looked. The Seven were gone, but everyone could still see the perfect rainbow.

I could feel that the ceremony had generated this rainbow, that the ceremony had asked for a sign, and the sign had come.

Jim leaned over and murmured, "I guess you know this is a fertility child Fire Starring ceremony aimed at you, don't you?"

I shook my head no. What was he talking about?

"They'll probably want you to go to the center and sing or pray or get prayed over in a minute."

At first, I figured he was kidding. But then I saw he looked quite serious. And I was suddenly horribly apprehensive. So I ducked out. I snuck behind the circle of people and slipped quickly well into the woods.

When I felt I was far enough away, I sat down under a large tree to think. It was quiet there, serene. There were luminous patches of snow on the ground, each one giving off its own white light which floated upward between the trees like a soft chalky flame.

I almost had a heart attack when I heard a voice grunt. I turned. Fire Star was sitting under my same tree. How had he found me? How had he gotten there so quickly and quietly? I made a move to push myself off the ground and leave. He put his hand down on mine hard, and refused to let me stand up. I glared at him.

He didn't let go and started to speak. "When snow gets very deep, and you are very cold, you can make your way in next to a big tree trunk. The tree will always keep you warm."

"Oh," I said coldly, but I noticed I was interested. His hand was still pressing mine into the ground. My palm started to hurt.

"There will be a time when you may need to know this. Are you ready for that time?"

"Don't know."

"I have seen that the Earth will one day be covered with spider webs. I have seen people looking for food, for warmth, for their own families, and even for death. I have seen you teaching them, leading them, showing them a new Ghost Dance to do on both sides. You will be doing this more and more as we move to the time … the opening."

He paused and looked at me. He could see that I was trying to look like I wasn't listening. He leaned toward me intently. "Listen. This is important. I have seen you delivering the people into the spirit realm. You must know this."

Some sort of bell went off in my head. As angry at him and repulsed by him as I was, I had to stiffly ask him, "You think it's coming? The big Earth change?"

"You know as well as I do," he warned, "it will come -- eventually."

I began to cry. "But why?' I was starting to believe all this, even though I didn't want to. Or, had I already known all this long ago?

"Because the Great Rebalancing is so much needed."

"This will be very awful, won't it?"

"It will be years and years from now, but it is time to begin to prepare the people. You know, on some level you know. This is why you have arrived here. You do know."

"No, please, I don't want to know."

"But you do know. You are supposed to know. We have seen that you will be a teacher of this knowing."

"Really?"

"Yes, this Earth change lore, wisdom, carries the Earth change truth. Earth change has come before and it will come again. The Great War will upset *Maka* and then *Maka Shan*, and all the *Maka Skhan*. When is not clear yet, but it will come again. *Maka Shan*. Maka. Maka."

I could feel he was in earnest, but I just shrugged. This was too big a thing for me to want to know right then. And, I wanted to believe, maybe I did believe, that there was another way things could go.

He pressed my hand even harder into the ground. I could feel the little stones cutting into my flesh. "Do not hide from what the Earth is saying to you, Akashakana. Do not close your ears because you are not liking me. I am just a pitiful old warrior. And you are cutting my heart with your baby teeth, young white wing medicine woman." He pressed my hand still harder. "My heart bleeds because of you."

I looked at him fiercely. "Let go of my hand. Never touch me again."

"Not yet," he answered sternly. "You have to listen."

I sent him a venomous look. "Let go."

We locked our harsh gazes. I didn't move, or blink, or glance at my hand even though my hand was starting to shoot hot pain up through my arm. Suddenly Fire Star lightened the pressure on my hand just a little and cleared his throat. He looked just a bit humble. "What do you think … Fire Star, he has not lived up to your wishes?"

I tried to pull my hand away, but he wouldn't let go. I couldn't stop my words. "No. He has failed me. He has failed his people. All people. All Earth."

Fire Star blinked. "Is that what you see? You see only what you want to see, not what is."

"I see the truth. This is what I know. The truth about you, Chief Fire Star."

"Akashakana, my young goddess, you are indeed breaking my heart. Don't you see I love you now?"

I was surprised. Could he really mean this, this thing about loving me now? I decided to stay cold. "No, I don't see this."

"Yes, you do, you see this and you feel this. You are my woman, and I love you."

"You do not love me. You want to control me."

"Why not be mine. Being the Chief's woman is an honor. You will like it."

"No I won't like it."

"I ask you again, have I not lived up to your wishes? As a leader and as a man?"

"I say again: You have failed me. On both counts."

Fire Star looked raggedly forlorn, actually hurt and broken, for just a moment. There was almost a tear forming in his left eye. "My priestess, I have wounded you. ... But I was called to take you like that. Called. ... But I hurt you, didn't I?"

I began to cry.

He watched me, unsure of what to do for a moment. Then he reached over as if he would hug me.

I pulled as far away as I could, but he still was pressing my hand down into the ground.

"Come close to me. Let me heal this, Akashakana. Let me," he almost pleaded.

I continued to resist him.

So he recovered his rough façade. "Well, young woman, you are wrong to be this way with me. You cannot know what you say. You cannot know what is right. White pain, and white knowing never did white people any good. In fact, it's killing all life on this Earth."

He tried again to pull me closer to him. He seemed almost desperate now.

I was able to yank away. I stood up and looked back down at him. "I suppose you thought I would trade my soul for what you think of as *your* teachings?"

"No. But you have been permitted entry into the sacred spirit realm of my people. You have been admitted into the inner circle of this Tribe. For this you make a trade."

189

"I don't need your admission to this Tribe. It's not your Tribe." I heard myself talking rather stridently and told myself to keep quiet. But I went on. "You don't rule this Tribe, you only think you do. You don't control Earth change knowledge; you only tell your people you do."

Fire Star frowned at me. "I see why your mother called you Lilith. She knew you. Look, you have been given a few sacred teachings. And already you think you are a medicine man. And you are only a woman. You think you have a right to the sacred realm, that it is your kingdom. You think you can take over for ME? Ho ho."

"You don't own the sacred teachings." I had no idea what I was getting at. "They belong to everyone. And leave my mother out of this."

"You have been allowed, woman Lilith, into this sacred territory … this survival nest. We are building the real Eden. Forget the teachings of your Judeo-Christian world. Come into your native blood. We know what all this is really about. We know the real teachings."

"I have --"

He interrupted. "You have been given the beginning keys to surviving the coming Earth changes. Now you will return the trade … you will stay here and protect the life of my son."

He pointed to my belly.

"No," I said and then went silent, carrying on a conversation with myself: If there is a trade to return, I will return it my own way. If there is something to give back, I will live in service of good. I will decide what good is. I will keep my own counsel about this. I have a right to access the sacred. These are my powers too. I --

He narrowed his eyes and interrupted my internal voice. "Your life depends upon this. You follow my law in my land, woman. I can love you, or harm you. Both are possible. Let me love you, you will be my queen goddess. Say no, well …"

I shivered inside. Was he threatening me, I wondered. Yes, he was, I told myself. "No. You cannot hurt me again. Not for the teachings, not for the land. This is everyone's land, not yours. And, I am not afraid of you or of your magic," I said, my voice suddenly resonating with a strange force surging within me, protecting me from him. "I have my own magic, and it's stronger than yours."

"You really think so, do you young she-star?"

I really did, but did not know why. "Yes, Fire Star, or whoever you really are, I do."

He relaxed his frown a bit, reached up and took my hand, almost paternally. "I am the father of your child, Lilith Akashakana. You will please honor me."

I blinked back the hot tears racing into my eyes. How could I respond to this unfair request from my assailant? "Honor you? You dishonored me. You hurt me. You raped me. You just about killed me. How do I honor that?" I was crying again. Somewhere out there, I heard the Seven say, the universe was not founded on rape.

He squeezed my hand, and then said in a surprisingly soft and disturbingly compelling voice, "You forgive me, because you are an angel, a great white wing angel, and you let me touch you again. You let me make love to you gently. Let me give you the pleasure you deserve."

I looked down at him, first in absolute shock, and next, as if he were out of his mind. Who was he really, other than a creature here for a while on this planet, a soul passing through? I had to wonder. In that moment, I knew that my love for Mother Earth had grown so much during my time with the Tribe. My whole world view had changed, but not exactly in Fire Star's direction. But now, I could not hate even my enemy. … I looked at Fire Star with empathy.

Fire Star felt my momentary opening of spirit. He went on, "We have a new Tribe to protect, you and I. We have knowledge to preserve into the future. This is why we have come together. This is not an easy meeting for us, but it would have been even harder if you had been older. … You are young, but you can learn. You were sent to us. I want you and our son by my side."

Son? I now thought to myself. Such arrogance that he thinks he knows this. Daughter if anything, I insisted silently.

Now he looked such a mix of humble and powerful, sincere and manipulative, I cringed. "How dare --" I blurted out anyway.

"Wait, Akashakana, wait to answer me. Go think and feel first. Listen to the spirit of the great Maka, my Akashakana. You will hear you are to join me. THIS IS THE MESSAGE OF OUR TIMES, THIS IS EARTH TALKING TO US."

Speechless, I pulled myself away from this unnerving exchange – unnerving because I was torn regarding the whole message from the Earth thing. Did I have a right to say no to a crying planet? Or was all this not something Fire Star should be involved in?

I turned, and walked away. I tried hard to figure out the meaning of this bizarre encounter. My heart was torn a thousand ways and I felt immensely confused. The walk back to camp was longer than the steps it took to get there. The distance was the struggle inside me plus the reality that I had to accept. But I needed to decide what that reality was in order to accept it.

When I got back to camp, I asked around for Kiowa, and found out that he was gone. Mark, who had been beginning to wonder what was going on between me and Kiowa, was happy to tell me that Kiowa had come to him quite gravely. Kiowa had told him to take care of me, to cherish me, to revere and protect me, or someone else would come along who would.

My heart shattered into billions and billions of irreparable fragments, pieces of me. Kiowa had left? Without saying goodbye to me? I would never get over this. And on some level, even years later, a part of me never did.

No words could express my pain. I was absolutely devastated. I knew deep down inside I would never see him again. Not in the flesh. Why? Why?

That night I decided to leave the Tribe, right away. I didn't say goodbye to anyone. I didn't take my things. I knew I'd have to travel light.

The moon was out and I could see the dirt road. I followed it for what felt like several hours. But it was a futile trip. I could feel that

I was being stalked. The ground told me. And sure enough, those same somber men that had greeted me when I first arrived at this place with Gun leapt out at me from behind a tree. As usual they were armed.

Now I saw their truck had been hidden way off the road, as if they had expected me to try to leave on foot that night. "Get in," the biggest one said.

I looked at him unusually calmly, close to the way I thought Singing Brook would. "No," I said.

"Get in."

"No," I said. "You can't make me."

He put the end of his rifle right in front of my face, an inch away.

I tensed. "You wouldn't shoot."

He cocked the trigger and then pushed the rifle tip into my pregnant belly. Another one of the men ordered, "Stop. Be careful with her." This one grabbed me by the shoulder, and pushed me toward the truck. I got in. What could I do?

They took me back to the land.

After that, there was always at least one of them nearby, holding a rifle and watching me. Everyone seemed to know I had tried to get out. The men with the rifles wouldn't let people come to speak to me. I was cut off from Singing Brook, and Osala, and Flower and Tree Dog, and Mark and Jim, and there was no Kiowa.

Fire Star made it clear he was waiting for my response.

Waiting.

We were all waiting for the Great War to begin, not seeing ourselves already deep within it.

Maka! Can you help us? Can you save us?

Maka! Bring me a way out of this madness, or out of what ever this may be.

16.
hard wave

I was escorted, if you can call it that.

I was brought to the next ceremonial gathering by one of the rifle-bearing men. He made me sit right next to Fire Star. I did so very stiffly. Fire Star was insulted and furious, I could tell. He had let down his guard. He had, in his way, apologized and asked for my heart and a partnership in Earth change, Maka Shan, teachings, and I had made him no reply. Or had I replied that I would take on the teachings, learn what these really were, and teach in my way? But that I would not be his woman? I wasn't sure.

I looked around, trying to meet the eyes of someone who would understand me. No one would make eye contact. I kept trying to find someone who would look at me. Finally, I met the eyes – or should I say I was found by the eyes – of a strange visitor, an intensely serious medicine woman who seemed to have an unusual kind of anger for me. I thought maybe this was jealousy she was beaming at me, but there was something bigger than this being expressed. She looked at me severely from across the circle. She seemed to hit me with her look – with the power of her look she seemed to be hexing me, to be giving me the evil eye. At least I thought it was evil. Maybe it was something else.

A hard wave raced at me – right out of her eyes. She shot a sharp arrow of searing energy at me. A hot pain hit my uterus. I crumpled.

No one came to help me. … When I could stand, I left the circle, stumbling off alone. No one followed. With every step, the arrow of pain became more focused in my womb. I tried to call Kiowa. But I couldn't concentrate. More pain. Cruel pain. Shocking waves of it. This angry medicine woman – is she turning the knife? Killing my baby?

The baby! My baby! But I love this baby. I love this baby. Too late. Is it too late? Now what? Kiowa where are you? I curled up under a tree and tried to call Kiowa. But I couldn't concentrate. I felt like I was shedding skin, the way a snake sheds its skin, but that the skin I was shedding was my body. After about an hour of convulsions, I realized I was shedding the baby's body. Was I dying too, as Fire Star had said would happen if I lost this baby? It seemed so. I was bleeding to death.

A few hours later I had completed this miscarriage. I lay still on the ground, wondering what to do next. I was too weak to move. I felt awful. *Mother Earth take me. Send me home ….*

But my baby needed safe passage. I instinctively knew this to be true. I prayed right then and there for guidance with this responsibility.

A little breeze came up and swept over me, like a blanket. I felt a hand touch my face. I looked up and saw Sveeka, the spirit of my mother in ancient form, a few feet away, holding my baby all bundled in an animal hide – a white piece of animal hide. She showed me the child and I heard her tell me, "This is your young priestess. She is of our lineage, too. She will come to you again when you are older and know better who you are." As she spoke, I saw this strong sweet being as a young adult, and then as a mature adult.

"But I am dying right now too," I whispered.

"Yes and no," Sveeka told me. "This transformation feels like physical death. But, you will live so very many more years here on this Earth to see your child come into this world, and to train her for her immense role, and to watch her move into her role over time. Many more years." Immense.

I came to understand that this child was indeed a girl child, and that she would someday be my daughter. Sveeka nodded at me and a wave of love came over me like an ocean of comfort.

I will protect this soul till you are ready, I heard Sveeka tell me. She is with me.

Then the breeze came up around her and she and the baby's spirit were off and heading for the time when I would be ready – when time would be ready.

I scratched a hole into the ground with my fingernails and a stick I found near me. There I placed the remains of the baby's body. While this was hard for me, I had the distinct feeling that the baby lived on and this was just a cleanup process here in the physical plane. I sang softly for the spirit that was carried off, off for the time being.

Cleaning up was suddenly very important to me. I tried to stand up but hurt too much. So I decided to crawl to the nearby stream to wash myself. It was difficult to move. The pain was unbelievable. I just about gave up trying to get to that stream when I remembered that I had told Kiowa how I'd seen that like rushing water nothing moves.

He had said, "exactly," as if I'd figured out a key to a puzzle or something.

So I put myself into that *stillness is motion and motion is stillness* state of mind and let the stream come to me. After a while, there it was.

I let the water purify me of the event. Then I stood myself up and made my way toward the barn where I'd been sleeping. On my way, I started hemorrhaging profusely. I went – practically crawling – looking for the people there who were my friends. But I couldn't find them. Singing Brook was gone. Mark and Jim were nowhere. I went to various other people for help, to whomever I could find, but I couldn't get any one to get me a ride to a hospital. They looked away from me when I tried to talk to them. They watched me suffer and ignored me. I was far too weak to walk out to the highway, although I considered trying.

I made my way to the barn, leaving a trail of blood and life force.

This problem continued. After about a week of bleeding, I found I was fainting every time I took more than ten steps.

Fire Star heard about what had happened. He called off the armed escort. He told Mark and Jim that I would stop bleeding if I had a lot of sex. So Mark kept forcing himself on me while I was passed out. He told Mark that other men should have sex with me, too.

I told Mark this was abuse and not to make it possible for Fire Star to command men to have sex with me. Thankfully, Mark seemed to agree, but I was too faint to tell for sure. The way I was being treated changed. Not that people were very nice to me before this happened. I was already being followed and ostracized for not stepping up to the throne of carrying the chief's chosen heir child. Now I was isolated and ignored, hated from a distance.

"Please, Mark, you have to believe me. I'll die if I stay here. Please."

"But I thought you didn't mind dying," he replied. "At least that's what you've always told me."

"Being free to chose my own way of dying is different from this. Mark, you don't want my death on your conscience. Get me out of here."

I prayed for someone to come and help. I heard the Seven speak deep inside my head: "Help yourself. Call the help to you … it will come."

I called help to me in every voice I had. It was a little like learning to ride a bicycle. Finally, I caught my balance, and then I knew my calling was heard. A divine circuit closed and the energy of my plea moved.

Help came the next night. It was simple and quick. A schoolteacher, or at least someone who said he was a schoolteacher, came up to the land, surprising everyone. He said he had suddenly had a bit of free time, had some friends up there on the tribal land, and had gotten the sudden urge to bring some food to donate to the Tribe. While the people were consuming with great zest the food he brought, he took a walk alone, to be with the land, he told them.

He found me semi-conscious on the barn floor. He seemed to know all about me. I don't know how. I don't know how he got me to his car later in the night. I was in and out of full awareness.

I remember being surprised when we got to the car. Mark and Jim were there. They were very worried about me. The schoolteacher seemed to be telling Mark and Jim what to do. They wrapped me in blankets and laid me down on the back seat. Mark, Jim and the teacher or whoever he was sat in the front seat. Mark kept checking on me as the teacher drove us out, off the land, and down the long dirt road.

I heard them talking.

The teacher said, "It's just by chance I was able to get you kids out tonight."

Mark and Jim actually seemed grateful, which surprised me.

I think I held my breath – afraid I would get sent back to the Tribe – until we were on the highway. And then I blacked out, soaking in my blood, and in what seemed, in my semi-conscious mind, to be the bloodshed of women throughout time.

I woke up being rolled into the hospital. I heard the teacher say, "You'll be okay. The worst is over now." I opened my eyes to see him looking down at me. "All you need is a little medication. Sometimes white man has the answer. Sometimes."

The schoolteacher held something before my eyes, making sure I could see it. I focused on it – a little white leather medicine bag, beaded with blue and ivory beads. And then he stuffed it into my palm and closed my fingers tightly around it. "Keep this. Always. It is from Kiowa. It holds his heart. Always and forever, he is yours, he told me to tell you. He loves you through all time. He told me to tell you that you are on the right path but that that tribal leader Fire Star is not. He told me to tell you to watch out for false prophets from now on, all your life. Kiowa also said I should tell you to follow the way of the *Wazine Maka Shan*. You know them, as you are of their lineage. Ask Sveeka. And he said I should repeat these words to you: '*Sayeth my name ... sayeth my name ... sayeth my name.*' "

I blacked out hearing the teacher saying these words again and again in mind.

Sayeth my name ... sayeth my name ... sayeth my name.

It is done.

Maka Shan.

epilogue:
unveiling the journey

The pilgrimage to self I report in this book began in 1970 with a ritual rape and strangling that I would have preferred to forever forget. But trauma and insight are strange bedfellows, and my life has been abundant with both. I wouldn't wish on anyone the difficult situations I have encountered, although what happened to me and more is part of many people's life experience. I would, however, wish upon all who desire it, the abundance of joy, love, light, spiritual revelation, and remarkable encounters with sacred teachings – both ancient and modern – with which I have been blessed.

These precious openings and ascensions have made my Earthly journey very rich and eternally unforgettable. I am deeply grateful to the master teachers and mystic guides – of both sexes and of all races and ages and religions – who have shared their knowledges with me. This includes the many members of the Native American and other Indigenous Peoples' communities who have taken me in and helped me to integrate the visions and spiritual experiences I, and others like me, have been having since childhood.

As the man called Gun, who comes into my life in the early part of this book, once told me, "wisdom does not always come to you in shiny gift wrap tied with pretty ribbon." Sometimes we must be roughly stripped of our veils, or recognize that we have been, by whatever means present themselves, to finally realize our purposes here. At least for me this has been the case. I certainly haven't found being on this planet always easy, in fact, it virtually killed me several times.

But each time I almost died, as I have written in this book, it seemed (against the odds) I was sent back – yes, strangely enough sent back by the Wazine Seven – by the Wazine Women, apparently ancestors of mine. These Seven ancient spirits, who I have become increasingly aware of (against most present day intellectual odds) have several times reminded me of who I am and why I am here at this particular historic moment in Earth time. I'm here around the *Maka Shan*, as are so many others.

I spent many years keeping relatively quiet about my apparently far beyond this reality, extra-dimensional, origins and contacts. I was especially careful not to reveal too much to "outsiders" (who ever they were) about my ongoing emergence into certain spirit realms. Many of these realms remain familiar to members of various indigenous and other groups around the world, groups who have not assimilated too far into the now 21st century modern denial culture. For the first two decades of my adulthood, I walked in at least two worlds, but I was quiet about this. And then, I grew quieter and quieter as time went by, as I felt I had a professional reputation to protect.

Then, to the great surprise of my family and colleagues, this deeper aspect of my Work was made, almost entirely by chance, public knowledge. The consequent shock waves were heavy; they kicked off an avalanche of profound transition in my life – an avalanche still in process. (See future volumes of this Maka Shan Saga for more on this.) And after being asked repeatedly, especially in recent years, by various publishers to talk openly about the inter-dimensional elements of my life, I have now clearly received the call to speak in depth about the blunt truth that has both plagued and blessed my current life experience: I don't come from this time, and ultimately, did not come originally from this planet. And this is true for many of us here, not just for me.

Quite distinct from what we try to assume are only human Earth origins, I am fully aware that I come from the intergalactic human grouping called Wazine, originating from the Freeborn Triton branch, an ancient arm of feminine humanity whose home planet was long ago exploded in a galaxy four quadrants and Seven zerahtz away. We are nomads now, dedicated to the preservation of the great endangered species of "conscious-energetic" soul that humanity has developed here on Earth and elsewhere.

What you, we, Earth humans do with your, our, evolution right now is critical, to all of us everywhere in all dimensions of existence. And I am here again, along with others, maybe even along with some of you readers, to help explain the deeper situation in which you, we, are currently gripped – and also to encourage a simple revolution of cosmic proportions. This revolution is already underway. This revolution will bring about the Great Return of truth.

So I have been required, as have many others here now, to commit to the full gamut of earthly emotion as you know it – riding your bodily-based emotional waves even more intensely than many of you choose to do, in order to help turn the tide working against the further evolution of conscious soul. Being raped and at certain levels even killed; having to heal from dangerous conditions; falling in love and as a result experiencing a deep ripping wound in the emotional body the likes of which I never have to experience when I'm not in the physical plane; experiencing the fierce social stigma leveled against those of us beings who know we are from elsewhere and admit it – experiences like these have made this physical plane journey quite intense.

There are those who are so enmeshed in the strict caricature of the face of contemporary consensual reality that, for those persons, there is no doubt, no question, no counter flow of evidence. And this is all right with me. They can see or not see what they want to see or not see. Yet, if I have ever stood among them, I am no longer one of them. In fact, I haven't been one of them for quite a while. At least a few eons.

There is a realm, a power, a sphere of energies and a matrix of intelligence, beyond our everyday modern automobile-television-computer-text message-popcorn scene. I believe we know this on an instinctual level. But only a series of invitations, triggers, and yes, sometimes traumas, will propel us into the investigation of what lies beyond. I will not say that I am fortunate. I am not pleased to say that I began my adulthood with a bizarre and presumably compromising experience that may have colored much of my life. On the other hand, doors opened for me in the wake of that experience, perhaps out of necessity, perhaps out of grief, perhaps out of trauma. Doors opened that I do not regret having walked through. And now I, and we, can hold these doors open for others who may want to walk this way, for others who may be called to walk this way, perhaps more protected, perhaps more aware of what this journey is, perhaps wanting company on the path....

We all know that life can be sublime and enchanting and life can be hard and sad. We must keep on keeping on, mustn't we? A trauma can ruin a life or it can be mastered and understood for its opportunity. Fire Star took from me that which was not his to take – my body. He tried to take my soul. He almost took my life.

Tribal elders have explained to me that his effort to squelch my eventual power backfired. In raping me, he weakened himself and lost much of his power to me, and to women he was doing this to, and to women of all races and places and times. He pursued me, trying to retrieve what he had lost when he raped me, but to no avail. For a long time, I had no idea – no conscious idea – what he was after.

I didn't understand any of this for years. Not really. I tried to erase the event from my mind, from my flesh, from my soul – to no avail. You see, denial only makes the effect of the memory worse.

After the rape I describe at the opening of this book, time went by. I got over it, so to speak, and began to want to hide the fact that it had happened. I did a pretty good job for a while. Once I denied as thoroughly as I could that it had happened, it took me years to look at the event again – to even admit to myself I had been raped.

I found myself in a family law class listening to the definitions of rape from a legal standpoint. I was moved to ask the professor, during a break, out of earshot of all the other students, "What about intercourse at gun point, when the loaded gun is held and aimed and then put down but kept pointed, aimed, enforcing the expectation of submission?"

The professor looked at me querulously and said, "Why, that is rape, my dear."

I must have looked taken aback, but I tried to look nonplused as I asked, "What is the statute of limitations, then?"

"Ten years, in most cases." I think he saw me calculating in my head the time that had passed, but I said only, "Thanks."

He started to say something forceful, I could tell, but then he caught himself and mumbled only, "You're welcome. Let me know if you have any other questions."

"Sure," I nodded and walked away.

I had found what I needed to find: The fact that this was indeed rape, and that any excusing it I might do was not going to erase the fact that this was rape.

It took me a lot longer to find out that others, other women, were suffering with, or at least carrying, the same memories – some even by the same man. Some by other self-proclaimed great teachers.

It also took me quite a while to recognize the commonality of my experience – and that of Fire Star's as well:

When a medicine man rapes a woman, he loses his power to the woman.

When a woman is forced into a position of no power by a man with power, eventually he will find his power leaves him and goes to her.

How long and when the exchange will be complete is the question. Does the woman need to see that this has happened? Does an eon or two have to pass first? Can a woman come into the power rightfully women's in her Earth life time? Today yes, the time has come, and this is the Turn we have been waiting for.

****

The time has come – and has come most urgently – to teach the people of the planet the techniques for overriding ecological and planetary disaster and for bringing peace, harmony, prosperity, and spiritual advancement to humanity. DON'T WE KNOW THIS?

And don't we see the global revolution brewing? Don't we know the build-up to the Great War is here? Don't we know we can still change the future? Don't we FEEL the need for the rise of the real feminine power? Can we survive without her magic?

Don't we feel what we need to do – register the need and express it deep in our bones? How can we walk around like robots, asleep and unaware? Are we already so far gone? Have we been that effectively blinded by our programming? We MUST break free of the shackles of our ignorance. Is it possible to have a voice into the mainstream mind?

If you are like me, you're getting the message more and more every day. Truth comes into focus as one's vision adjusts – as the arbitrary lines between fiction and reality, myth and truth, prophecy and history, disappear. Then critical and otherwise unrecognized information makes itself known in astonishing ways.

This has certainly been the case with the story I tell here. This is the coming of age, the coming into focus, the emerging deep into our hearts, of an uncanny sense of Truth. This is the clarification of the metaphor of split brain – of the crippling divergence in the evolution of the human mind that took place long ago – yes, a gender divergence. More aptly stated, a diversion of power from one gender to another, utilizing agents of evolutionary enhancement.

I am not talking about eliminating the masculine. I am talking about halting our lip service to the feminine and getting at what it really is. The reason is simple: If we don't do this, we die out.

When the fractured human consciousness – which is currently represented by the native peoples and (or versus) the modern civilizations – pulls itself together, then humans will be a potent force in many dimensions of reality. We are being watched at this juncture in our evolution. There are those who seek to enable this reunion of our fractured consciousnesses and there are those who seek to obstruct it.

What does this say about men and women? That they must learn to exist in a new world order for there to be any world order with the potential to survive the coming challenges we as a species will pose ourselves.

And the portals to the spirit realm – dare we shut them off? Dare we seal them for good with the scars of modern denial? The keepers of deliverance, the priestesses, the Isises of birth and death – they know the meaning of the entry way. They know that the demise of access is the demise of life in all dimensions. They know exile and they know the Great Return.

This knowledge has made its way into my heart, by force of its will, by contract through time. I have grown accustomed to the voices of the Seven ancient priestesses. I have come to understand their – our – mission.

So now, when the magic flies in, it no longer stuns me. When I lift out of this gravity, I am no longer disoriented. After all, weightlessness is a reasonable experience in outer space ….

Maa-Kah-hoh Tehrr-ha, vozhlahz wo, mee skhan-hey-yah.

Mother Earth, take me, send me home….

Maka

Maka

Maka Shan

afterword
by
dr. angela browne-miller

This is the first volume of the Maka Shan Saga. *Maka Shan* is the journey of a young woman in search of self. Yes, she wants truth, meaning, purpose, and survival knowledge, but she also wants self. Such a central part of the human journey, the drive for survival and the search for self....

Here, in this coming of age and spiritual quest story, our heroine (or subject) stumbles into clashings and meshings of ancient and modern teachings, mythologies and wisdoms. She actually seeks the truth about predictions of coming Earth changes, and travels far and wide to find this. Everywhere she turns, she hears that the time of great change is coming. In fact, the book opens with her coming involuntarily into a situation where she is believed to be among those chosen to bring survival teachings to the people of this planet. She is confused and troubled by the pressure she feels, pressure to take on such work.

Whether or not we follow earth change mythologies and beliefs, we are all on this quest for survival together. This is a species thing, and also a personal thing. We are all on our own personal quests, individual lifetimes, yet on these together. And we all know the range of challenges out there, on the life journeys we travel alone and together.

We can therefore tap into the experience of the main character in this book, our heroine. In fact, here our heroine, or subject, might also be called our victim or survivor, as she struggles to recover from a rape. This rape is both literal and metaphorical, even symbolic.

This is, perhaps, not the form of rape we tend to hear most about, but another form of rape, a more difficult to discern rape. In this instance, the person committing the rape presents himself as a great teacher, as the keeper of ancient and sacred survival knowledges. While rarely addressed, this form of rape, a too frequently excused and or ignored ritual rape, is quite prevalent, and quite dangerous. It is also quite confusing for the victim or survivor of this rape, because access to knowledge, or in this case to what are presented as sacred teachings, appears to be carried by the person raping. In this instance our heroine believes that the rapist does carry important sacred teachings. However, she comes to realize that she can access these teachings without the rapist's help. And in fact, this is the time in our history, in our times, when the emerging feminine teachings carried into the now from ancient eras are available to us via other routes.

Whatever the challenges we face in our lives, we are driven to withstand and even rise above these. For some, a story, a myth, or an actual revelation fuels our survival. We are strengthened, fortified by our ways of placing our experiences into the context of the larger picture....

We're like old bottles collecting on an old stone wall. In the storms, some of us break, some of us are shattered. But we can stand up again, resurrect our selves and be among those left standing – standing a little lonely because a great part of the journey is solitary and glassy, but standing nevertheless. Yes, we are still standing, and together.

As we weather such things, we quicken our souls, we deepen. We become so very transparent when we have died and survived. We grow so knowing when we have been shattered and then have pulled ourselves together again. We grow strong as we come to see that we are not the vessels (even the sometimes abused vessels) we live in, we are the spirits within – and without.

Taking this knowledge into the quest for the truth regarding our personal and species survival may be a large matter, an immense undertaking. Nothing minor drives those who seek to know the meanings of the ancient and modern Earth change teachings. We feel something calling us, and some of us listen. Whether or not we like it, something has worked its way into our collective consciousness or unconsciousness – whichever we choose to call this. What is this we sense? What is it we know or believe we know?

Whatever it is defined as being, there is a collective unconscious. Or perhaps this is a collective subconscious, with strands of realization seeping into our awareness in bits and pieces, and in waves. This collective mind or soul speaks to us, brings to us messages and keys to existing, to living, to survival. Best we listen. Best we hear.

Sometimes critical – essential – information can only percolate to the surface of human consciousness in story or fantasy form. Were it to come in as fact, it might be too bizarre, startling or overwhelming to believe. It might be too big to recognize. This is why we can be presented with sign after sign and still not see. And so we are blind to the significance of what flashes before us while we blink in denial and fear.

Not seeing may have become a way of life for far too many. We may be receiving important information that we are not hearing. The challenge is then, to open our eyes, take as much as we can in, and be quite careful in our discovering the difference between noise and information.

WHAT FOLLOWS THIS VOLUME, MAKA SHAN?

Volume Two of the
Maka Shan Saga:

THE
GREAT RETURN
BY
ANATARRA WHITE WING

(See cover on next page)

This is the story of a young woman, Lilith Akashakana, whose life has somehow been pulled into a mysterious journey. This is the journey of everyone on the quest for truth about what is really going on now, here on Earth, in our times. Are there ancient secrets that explain our times and the possibility of power shifts and even Earth changes to come? Who knows the truth about all this? And who has a right to access this truth? Lilith Akashakana is determined to access this information she believes is her, our, birthright. She travels to homes of ancient tribes such as the Mayans who know what she has been told is the true medicine and the true truth.

She has broken out of the normal path of life she had been expected to follow, and now is in search of meaning and truth, as well as of ancient survival knowledge teachings. Many events have taken place in her young life, including the recent death of her mother, and her being raped by someone who had access to the survival teachings she was so intent upon learning. Some sort of transfer of power has taken place, and Lilith is being called to know this.

This novel can be read free standing or as the sequel to Maka Shan, which is Volume One of this Maka Shan Saga. Volume One closes with our heroine barely surviving a strange form of captivity, and finally free. Now, in Volume Two, The Great Return, she embarks on a journey to understand the teachings she had absorbed during this very trying time. She finds out, much to her surprise, that there is an ancient tribe of medicine women seeking to come back into the now to influence the course of history and the fate of this Earth. They are calling her, and others like her now, in our times....

Find *The Great Return*, the sequel to *Maka Shan*, as a paperback on Amazon, and as an Ebook on Kindle:

THE GREAT RETURN

VOLUME TWO: MAKA SHAN SAGA

ANATARRA WHITEWING

Afterword by

Dr. Angela Browne-Miller

About the Author of
MAKA SHAN:
LIKE RUSHING WATER RUSHING MOVES
ANATARRA WHITEWING

Anatarra Whitewing is a spiritual advisor and theologist. She is a freelance reporter and author of several books under several pen names. As author of the Maka Shan Saga collection, she does write under the name Anatarra Whitewing:

Maka Shan Saga© Volume One:
Maka Shan©
Written by Anatarra Whitewing.
Afterword by Dr. Angela Browne-Miller.

Maka Shan Saga© Volume Two:
The Great Return©
Written by Anatarra Whitewing.
Afterword by Dr. Angela Browne-Miller.

Maka Shan Saga© Volume Three
(Title to be Announced)
Written by Anatarra Whitewing.
Afterword by Dr. Angela Browne-Miller.

Maka Shan Saga© Volume Four
(Title to be Announced)
Written by Anatarra Whitewing.
Afterword by Dr. Angela Browne-Miller.

Author Contact:
AnatarraWhitewing@Metaterra.com
Info@Metaterra.com

Books by the Author
of the
Afterword to this Book:
ANGELA BROWNE-MILLER

http://www.AngelaBrowne-Miller.com
Also uses pen name:
DR. ANGELA DEANGELIS
(See these and other books by this author listed on Amazon.)

Endings are Beginnings:
Navigating Your Hard Times Into Higher States
Written by Angela DeAngelis.

Embracing Eternity:
The Life Force Does Not Die
Written by Angela DeAngelis.

Transition and Survival Technologies:
Interdimensional Consciousness as Healing, Survival and Beyond
Written by Angela DeAngelis.

Healing Earth in All Her Dimensions:
Personal, Species and Planetary Healing
Written by Angela DeAngelis.

Rewiring Your Self to Break Addictions and Habits:
Overcoming Problem Patterns
Written by Angela Browne-Miller.

To Have and To Hurt:
Seeing, Changing or Escaping Patterns of Abuse in Relationships
Written by Angela Browne-Miller.
Foreword by Arun Ghandi.

Will You Still Need Me:
Finding Friends, Love and Meaning as We Age
Written by Angela Browne-Miller.
Foreword by Evacheska DeAngelis.

Raising Thinking Children and Teens:
Guiding Mental and Moral Development
Written by Angela Browne-Miller.
Foreword by Evacheska DeAngelis.

International Collection on Addictions
Dr. Angela Browne-Miller, Editor.

Violence and Abuse in Society:
Understanding a Global Crisis
Dr. Angela Browne-Miller, Editor.

ALSO
LOOK FOR THESE GREAT BOOKS
BY ANOTHER IMPORTANT
METATERRA AUTHOR:
ALIAS SKYE
http://metaterra.com/novelsbytitle.html

Bloodwin Saga Collection© Volume One:
Project Heartfire©
Written by Alias Skye.
Afterword by Dr. Angela Browne-Miller.

Bloodwin Saga Collection© Volume Two:
Bloodwin Manifest©
Written by Alias Skye.
Afterword by Dr. Angela Browne-Miller.

Bloodwin Saga Collection© Volume Three:
TO BE ANNOUNCED.

Akasha Saga Collection© Volume One:
Akasha Protocol©
Written by Alias Skye.
Afterword by Dr. Angela Browne-Miller.

Akasha Saga Collection© Volume Two:
Akashic Collapse©
Written by Alias Skye.
Afterword by Dr. Angela Browne-Miller.

metaterra®
publications

Maka Shan©, written by Anatarra Whitewing, is published by Metaterra® Publications for general distribution to readers all over the world. Metaterra® Publications is an independent publisher dedicated to the furthering of insight, wisdom, truth, learning, creativity, and perception. For other Metaterra® publications, see the Metaterra® website:

http://www.Metaterra.com

Metaterra® Publications also offers its historical fiction line.

**See Novels by Title Section
of the Metaterra.com website
and see also Amazon.com/
Look for:**
Proxy War© (Volume One: Phantom War© Trilogy)
by E.L. Speed
(January 2012).
and
Matumba's Legacy©
by E.L. Speed
(June 2012).

See also Metaterra® Publications by other authors:
Still Chattel©
and
Fiat Vox©: Let There Be Voice©

www.ingramcontent.com/pod-product-compliance
Lightning Source LLC
Chambersburg PA
CBHW071330250626
47159CB00004B/1540